Hardie Grant
EGMONT

Holy Crush A-moly!
first published in 2013
this edition published in 2018 by
Hardie Grant Egmont
Ground Floor, Building 1, 658 Church Street
Richmond, Victoria 3121, Australia
www.hardiegrantegmont.com

A catalogue record for this
book is available from the
National Library of Australia

Text copyright © 2013 Thalia Kalkipsakis
Illustration and design copyright © 2018 Hardie Grant Egmont

Design by Pooja Desai
Typesetting by Ektavo

Printed in Australia by McPherson's Printing Group, Maryborough, Victoria.

1 3 5 7 9 10 8 6 4 2

The paper in this book is FSC® certified.
FSC® promotes environmentally responsible,
socially beneficial and economically viable
management of the world's forests.

GIRL VS. THE WORLD

HOLY CRUSH A-MOLY!

THALIA KALKIPSAKIS

Hardie Grant
EGMONT

Chapter One

Three minutes might not seem long, but it can be long enough to change everything.

That's all the time it took for me to get with the wrong guy and end up with the whole school whispering junk about me. Three useless minutes.

But now we have to do public speeches in English, and I'm going to make my three minutes count. The whole class will be listening, so this is my chance to make an impression. A good one, this time.

When I first started at McEwan College, I didn't know

a soul. People used to stare through me as if I didn't exist, and when some of them did start to notice me it was only because they were gossiping about my crap taste in guys.

I don't know what I would have done without Briana. She just leant over in maths one day and asked what brand of conditioner I use. It may not sound like much but I could have kissed her, because Briana wasn't just chatting about split ends. She was letting me know that I wasn't stuck on my own forever. She was saving my butt, basically.

Usually I'm not a stressed-about-homework sort of person; I'm more of a sit-back-and-flick-through-my-fave-mag sort of girl. But when Mr Mendes told us about the public speaking assessment, I actually stopped doodling to listen.

'Speak for three to five minutes,' he said. 'And talk about something that's important to you.'

Maybe it was the way he paused before saying the word *important,* but straight away I knew my topic. Nothing else was even an option. My topic was something massive that hardly anyone knows about me. And if I could do a half-decent speech, maybe people would stop seeing me as the new girl who got with the wrong guy.

When I got home after school, I didn't flick through *Glamour Girl* once. Instead, I switched off my music, lay on my bed, and tried to work out how to put the most important thing in my life into a three- to five-minute speech.

At first I just lay there thinking, pen in hand. Where to start? But once I pressed the nib to the page, it all flowed out. This is one topic I can talk about for ages. I ended up with paper spread across my bed like a huge pile of white autumn leaves.

After dinner I collected the pages, reading through and crossing out bits here and there. Even after Steph came in to bed and I had to turn off the bedroom light, I kept working by the light of my lamp, writing key sentences onto cue cards to jog my memory.

It's late now, after eleven, but I think my speech is ready. It's the best I can make it, anyway. So I leave the cue cards on my bedside table, switch off the lamp and pull the doona over my shoulder.

But instead of falling asleep, I keep going over my speech in my head. Stuck in a three-minute repeat. But I don't care; I'm not even tired.

Mr Mendes wants to hear about something important to me. So that's what he's going to get.

The next thing I know I'm jolting upright with a gasp, freaked out by a stupid dream.

I was standing in front of the class, about to start my speech when I looked down and realised I'd forgotten to put on clothes. Even worse, I'd forgotten to shave. Ugh!

I flop backwards on my pillow. Check the clock: 6.57 a.m.

'Phoebs? You okay?' Steph is beside me, her hand on my forehead. 'Bad dream?'

I lift the covers so she can slide in beside me. Her toes snuggle against my thigh.

'Oh, man, that was awful,' I groan, and snort out a laugh.

'About Mum?' There's a pause as I shake my head, but she keeps going. 'It's okay. We don't have to worry anymore. She's okay now.'

It's sort of sweet and sort of sad, seeing her comfort me like this. Ever since Mum's been sick, Steph's been sleeping in my room. At first she slept in bed with me but once Mum was through the worst, Steph dragged in a fold-out mattress and announced that she was camping on the floor.

For the past nine months, Steph's been the one waking with a gasp every few nights, and it's been me saying over and over, *It's all right. Everything will be all right.*

I prop myself up on my elbow, resting my head in my hand. 'It was about my speech today,' I say. 'Not Mum.'

'So you're not worried about her? Really?' I can see her searching my face for any hint that there's still reason to stress, a clue that I might have hidden bad news from her.

'Nope, she's out of respite …' I begin slowly. 'She's staying with Aunty Celia for two more weeks …' I nod so that Steph joins in. 'And then she'll be home for good.' We chant the words together softly, like a prayer. As if saying them seriously enough makes them certain to happen.

Steph props herself up, copying my pose. 'Then everything will go back to normal.'

'Yeah.' But I can't look her in the eye. Normal? I'm not even sure what that means anymore.

Steph trots off to get dressed while I hit the shower. Hair first. While the conditioner's doing its stuff, I race the razor over my legs. Then I give my forearms a light shave, just to be safe.

Mostly I'm happy having a Greek dad – it's great having thick, dark hair and I like my dark eyes. The downside to having Greek genes, though, is turning into Gorilla Girl every night. If I didn't know how to keep it all under control, I'd end up with black hair everywhere. Like, *everywhere*.

I have the de-gorilla-fying routine down to a fine art, though. It's sort of soothing: a way of making sure I have it together, ready to face the world. While I work, I go over my speech in my head. I'll have the cue cards if I get stuck, but this 'doing your homework' thing isn't so bad. As it turns out, I pretty much know my speech by heart.

When I finish in the shower, I dry off, moisturise and

then find my uniform draped over the back of a chair in my room. Sigh. Talk about an old-lady outfit. But there are things you can do to make the uniform look a little better. Keep your skirt short, for a start, and lose the blazer whenever you can. Way to look like a sack of potatoes. And if you tuck your jumper up a couple of times at least it shows some shape.

No make-up. Yet. Dad would kill me if he knew about the magic bag of make-up tricks I sneak to school.

He nods when I wander into the kitchen. *'Pos kimithikes?'* he asks. 'How did you sleep?'

I shrug. 'Yeah, fine.' If I tell Dad I woke up stressing, he'll think it was about Mum.

'Lunches are done,' Dad says, still in Greek. 'And the washing machine's on.'

'Okay.' I grab an Up&Go from the fridge. 'I'll do the dishwasher,' I say and spike the straw into the silver hole.

'Kala.' Dad downs the rest of his coffee and checks his phone.

It's the routine we do every morning: Going Through The List. This is how it's been ever since Mum got sick.

We don't exactly talk about it, but it's as if we've dealt with it in the same way, me and Dad. The whole time Mum was seeing specialists and having operations, there was nothing we could do to help – we just had to trust the doctors, pray and wait. We're probably the world-record holders in waiting.

So much was out of our hands, but The List was something that we could control. We couldn't fix Mum, but we could make sure that Steph got to school each day. We could keep the house clean.

So that's what we focused on. For Steph, and for each other.

'I'll take care of dinner too, okay?' I say. Last item on The List.

'Real food, though,' says Dad. Which basically means Greek food.

I think for a bit. 'What about the pastitsio in the freezer? I'll do a salad too.'

'*Neh.*' Yes. He smiles, and the wrinkles around his eyes deepen. 'All under control, eh?'

'Always.' I grin back as Dad checks his watch.

'Time for me to go.' He kisses me on the forehead. *'Antio, koukla mou.'*

Dad heads over to the living area, lifts Steph up from the rug and swings her around until she screams, 'Daaaaaaad! Oh! Noooooo!'

He lowers her carefully to the floor, and then waits. I count down in my head: *tria, thio, ena …*

Steph lifts both arms in the air. 'Again! Again!'

Dad spins her one more time while I suck down the rest of the Up&Go. As always, he's wearing a tailor-made suit. He likes to keep fit so he looks pretty good. Well, pretty good for a businessman.

I'd never say it to him, but I'm proud of my dad. When he was nineteen, he packed a couple of suitcases, hugged everyone goodbye and jumped on a plane to Australia.

I can't imagine how freaky that would be, moving to some strange place you'd never been – like catching a one-way rocket to Mars. But the way he talks, it's as if it was no big deal. His English wasn't good back then, so he picked a finance course at uni that he knew he'd understand. He says numbers are a universal language. Now he works in a stockbroking company, so we're 'reasonably well off' (as he puts it). But it means he works long hours, which isn't so great.

Steph's back on the floor now, standing all wonky and going 'woooaaah' as if the world's a merry-go-round.

'I'll be home around seven,' Dad says in Greek, and grabs his briefcase. Then he turns back to me. *'Kali tychi me tin thialexis sou.'*

'Thanks, Dad.' He just wished me good luck with my speech.

At school, I duck into the girls' toilets and pull out my magic bag. Mascara, eyeliner and just a light tint for my lips. Without a bit of help, I'm totally plain and boring. When I walk out, my back is a little straighter. Ready to face the day.

I've just rounded the corner when I see Mr Chiu and do an immediate 180-degree turn.

Most teachers at McEwan turn a blind eye to a bit of eyeliner. They're the ones who are here to teach. Then there are the others who turn up desperate for their daily power trip. Like Mr Chiu.

Every morning Mr Chiu does a circuit of the school grounds, his arms swinging and his back straight as a robot's as he marches from one end of the school to the other, trying to catch anyone who makes the mistake of standing out as an individual. He's made me wipe off my make-up twice and I've had detention, too.

Not today. Sticking close to the wall, I slip the long way round B block and safely reach our meeting spot. Made it one more time.

Briana and Erin are busy talking as I walk up to the bench. I raise one hand in a wave. 'Hey!'

Two heads turn my way and Briana shoots me the best grin in the world. 'Phoebs, you're here!'

I'm about to slip in next to Bri when I change my mind and sit on the other side of Erin instead. It's safer this way.

'Hey, Phoebs,' Erin says with this half-smile as I settle in. She and Briana have been best friends since the beginning of time, so I've become a bit of an expert in not coming between them.

Briana kicks her feet under the bench nervously. 'So, ready for your speech?'

'Yeah, think so. I worked on it all last night.'

'Really?' They both do a double-take that cracks me up. Usually, I'm scribbling down homework at the last minute.

I flick a hand to make it seem like no big deal. 'I just didn't want to stand up there with my mouth gaping open like a fish for three minutes.'

'I wonder if Hamish is all right. He's really stressed about it,' Briana says.

Erin and I exchange a look. Briana is totally obsessed with Hamish, but she tries not to show it. 'You can go and talk to him if you want,' says Erin.

'Nah.' Briana swings her legs under the bench seat as if they're itching to get moving. 'I'll catch him in homeroom.' But two seconds later, she shifts in her seat. 'Actually, I'm going to check on Hamish. Then I'll come back, okay?'

'Off you go,' Erin says with a smile.

Briana springs out of her seat, but she's only made it a few paces when she stops and swivels. 'Sure?'

'Yes!'

We both laugh as Briana swivels again and this time makes it all the way to the end of A block.

For a while we just hang. Saying nothing. I search around for a topic to break the silence. Talk about needle-in-a-haystack territory. Erin likes computer games, sci-fi and fantasy, and she's really smart. She always vagues out if I bring up clothes or make-up. And that leaves boys.

'So, how are things with George?' I ask.

This topic, at least, I know she's into. Erin got together with a guy on her bus soon after Bri and Hamish hooked up. It's weird how life turns upside down. Not long ago, I was the only one in our group who'd even got with a guy, even if kissing Nelson was a huge mistake. But now I'm the only one who's single. It's okay, I guess. I mean, I'm not jealous or anything, but still. I wouldn't exactly complain if there was a guy in my life.

Erin smiles a little to herself. 'Yeah, he's okay. He's all worked up about this science camp he's going on next week.'

'Oh … right …' Then I go quiet. What do I know about science camp?

Erin leans back and crosses her ankles in front of her. If you look carefully, you can just see the hairs on her legs. Faint little dainty hairs. She doesn't even shave.

And me beside her, the Gorilla Girl. Not half jealous.

A minute later, Briana bounces back and announces that Hamish is in borderline meltdown about standing up in front of everyone.

Then first bell goes, and it's as if a switch has suddenly flicked inside me. My heart quickens and energy spreads through every cell in my body.

Just first period, recess and then it will be time for my speech.

Chapter Two

By the start of second period, everyone's on edge. Briana gets even bouncier than usual, which is saying something. I'm getting seasick just looking at her. Erin stays calm, but every now and then she clears her throat as if checking that her voice still works.

First up is Jagath. He always has to explain to people that his name's pronounced with a 'd' sound at the end. *Jagad*, I say to myself. No-one else seems to have noticed, but underneath that serious expression he's a total hottie. I've hardly spoken to him, but I've had a secret crush on him for months now.

The thing is, kissing Nelson last term ruined my life. It's taken me ages to feel okay about liking any guys again or telling anyone about it. But Jagath is the complete opposite to Nelson; he seems really nice.

He's got gorgeous dark, wavy hair and these amazing eyes with eyelashes most girls would kill for. He's Indian, I think. You can tell he's fit, but he's not a football type. He seems really smart and is always being called up at assembly for some award or other.

His speech is really passionate, all about the plight of orangutans in Borneo, and I even begin to imagine that he's saying it all to me. Like, we're the only two in the room. *Sigh* ... But about halfway through, the daydream freezes. Reality catches up with the fantasy.

All I know about primates is that I could potentially be mistaken for one if I didn't shave every day.

After Jagath's orangutans comes a boring speech on some famous footballer. Snore. Erin's talk is on Hero Quest, this online game she plays all the time. I've never played it, but I like what she says about the cool female characters. I wish I could escape to a world like that, sometimes.

Me next.

As soon as Mr Mendes calls my name, my heart kicks into a gallop. Clutching my cue cards, I step to the front of the class and scan the faces staring at me. My hand lifts to smooth my hair and I'm hit with a wave of second thoughts. My mouth opens, but no words come. All the other topics so far have been about people's hobbies and interests. But this is really personal. This is about someone I love.

'Whenever you're ready, Phoebe,' says Mr Mendes.

For something to do, I check my cue card for the first line. My breath gets this nervous wobble as I inhale and then slowly exhale. Now or never.

'On November the sixth last year, I came home to find an ambulance in front of our house.'

As soon as I say my first words, a hush comes over the room. Even the guys up the back stop drawing dumb pictures and listen.

I'm not nervous anymore. Now that I've actually begun, my words flow smoothly. I know the topic inside out; it's something I've thought about almost constantly for nearly a year.

I don't want to make people feel sorry for me, so I stick with the facts. But they're enough to make Erin's eyes widen, and Mr Mendes frowns.

Some personal stuff comes out too. The way Mum seemed to shrink in the hospital bed. Watching Dad break off in the middle of a sentence to blink away tears. And trying to be there for Steph when the person she really needed was Mum. What to tell her when even the doctors didn't seem to know what to say.

As I talk, I can sense the focus of the whole class on me. It's the strangest feeling. I hold on to their attention like a piece of string, pulling it tight and then, near the end, relaxing and letting it slacken.

For three minutes, I've taken them right inside my life.

When I finish the whole class claps, just as they've been doing for everyone. Maybe it's my imagination, but it seems louder this time. From the expressions on their faces, I get the sense that their applause is because of the happy ending: Mum's almost home now.

I float back to my seat, feeling lighter. Not just because I got through my speech, but because telling everyone means Mum's illness is coming to an end. I couldn't speak about it while she was sick – it was too scary. But now I can talk about it, so that must mean it's over.

The clapping dies as I take my seat. Briana leans close, putting a firm hand on my arm.

I worry for a moment. It was a relief to talk about it at last, but I hope people aren't going to treat me like some sob story now. I definitely don't want any fresh whispering to start.

Mr Mendes steps to the front of the class and clears his throat. 'Thank you, Phoebe, for sharing that with us. I'm glad your mother's out of hospital now.' Then he calls the next person up for their speech.

When the lunch bell goes, I'm hanging out for the break. I want to debrief with Briana and Erin and find out what they really thought about my speech. Good? Bad? Way too personal?

'Phoebe, could you come up here for a minute?' asks Mr Mendes. Inside, I groan. Being asked to see the teacher can mean only one thing in my world: bad news. He'd better not suggest I see the school counsellor or anything.

I mouth *save me* at Briana, but she smiles and squeezes my arm. 'Meet you at the bench,' she says.

I slowly make my way between the desks to the front of the room.

Mr Mendes takes his time, straightening a bunch of papers. He looks up and smiles. 'Well done today, Phoebe. I was impressed with your speech.'

Mr M pauses for my reaction, but I just check out the stuff on his desk, waiting to see where he's going with this.

'You were the only one in our class who paused regularly and made eye contact,' he continues. 'Did you feel the impact you were making?'

'Yeah, I guess.' For a second I glance up, remembering how it felt to hold everyone's focus.

Mr M nods encouragingly. 'I want you to know that your mark is the highest in our class.'

I'm filled with a strange flush of pride. Usually I'm called up for being late with an assignment, or making mistakes because I rushed.

'Maybe now you'll put in a bit more effort with the rest of your work. You never know what you could achieve,

Phoebe, until you try.'

'Yeah, ah … thanks,' I say, sure I've started to blush. Somehow, I don't even mind.

Mr Mendes nods to show I'm free to go. As I make my way out of class, each of my steps end with this happy little bounce. Top mark! I've never got top mark for anything. I can't wait to tell Dad!

I bounce out into the corridor, and almost crash straight into someone standing just outside the English classroom.

It's Jagath. This strange, surprised gasp comes out of me and I only just manage to pull up in time. My face is only millimetres from his chest.

I look up, gulp and step back. 'Hi,' is all I manage.

He clears his throat. 'Hey, glad I caught you.'

'Me?' I say, and my second blush of the day warms my face. Get a grip, Phoebe.

For some reason, being that close to his chest makes me imagine how he'd look with no shirt on. His muscles standing out …

'Good speech,' he says.

'Oh, thanks,' I say. I don't use his name, because I'll say it wrong for sure. Instead, I just smile while my heart pounds away a million miles an hour.

'I was wondering if maybe you'd join the junior debating team?'

'Oh … um … I've never really thought about debating,' I mumble at his hair. It's all windswept and wavy.

'Well, we're looking for someone new because our third speaker just moved away. Without three speakers, we don't have a team.'

I'm still checking out his hair when I get the sense that I've been quiet too long. I drop my eyes slightly to find him staring back at me.

Awkward.

'So, how about it?' he asks, one eyebrow raised.

I shake my head, floating slowly back to earth. As if a smart guy like Jagath would ever be interested in me. 'Thanks, but debating's not really my thing.'

'Really?' Jagath tilts his head to one side. 'Well, you don't have to decide right now. We've got a meeting on Wednesday. Maybe just come and check it out.' He's staring right at me. Like, really staring.

'I guess I could,' I say slowly.

'Great!' Jagath scribbles something on a piece of paper, folds it and hands it to me. 'Here's where we're meeting. See you then.'

As he walks away, I remember how good it felt to hold everyone's attention during my speech. Maybe I would be an okay debater? It's sort of nerdy, but Jagath would be there too ...

And I can't stop myself from smiling.

It's only when I dump my stuff in my locker that I check what the note says:

Library, study room 3A. Wed 3.30.

After school? That changes everything. Without Mum at home, I'm the only one around who can pick Steph up from school.

Could I sort out something with Dad? I carefully fold the paper and slip it into the side pocket of my backpack.

Grab my tomato sandwich. Slam the door.

The guy whose locker is right next to mine slams his at the same time. Our eyes meet, and we do this awkward kind of smile. When I first started here he used to stare right through me, but these days I think he's actually noticed that I exist.

I've almost finished my sandwich when I make it to our bench. Erin shoves along so I can sit in the middle.

'So, what did Mr M say?' asks Briana as I settle in.

'Um … just that my speech was … you know,' I shrug, 'all right.' Don't want them thinking I have a big head. Briana's not too good at English. Actually, she's not too good at any subject except PE.

'Just all right?' Briana cries. 'It was better than all right! I already knew most of the stuff you said and I still had this golf ball in my throat.'

'Even Bruce got all teary, did you see?' asks Erin. Bruce is a football meathead.

'And then the end …' Briana squeezes my knee. 'It's really great that your mum's going to be okay.'

'Yeah,' I say. 'Thanks.'

Briana settles back, sipping her juice pack. Erin's eyes stay on me.

'Your speeches were really good too,' I say, turning to Briana and then back to Erin. 'That stuff about the main female character in Hero Quest being so strong ...'

'You thought it was okay?' Erin leans forward. 'I mean ... it made sense?'

'Of course,' Briana says, except her nod turns into a kind of vague circular movement. 'Most of it.'

Still, Erin's watching me. 'Definitely,' I say. 'The way you compared it to other games with a guy as the hero ... it was cool.'

Erin smiles then, as if she's pleased about what I said.

We move on to Briana's speech after that, about her holiday up to Cairns, but I find myself checking back to Erin as we talk.

I feel as if I understand her better. Maybe we won't have to worry so much about awkward silences anymore. After our speeches today, we seem to have more in common.

I like this idea, so maybe that's why I say in the next pause: 'Guess what? Jagath asked me to join the debating team.'

'Hey, that's great!' Erin says straight away. 'You'll be really good.'

'Yeah, it's great, Phoebs,' Briana says.

'Really?' I turn from one to the other.

'Yeah. Your speech was really good,' Briana adds. 'No wonder they want you to join, represent the school and all that … No offence, but I didn't realise you were so smart.'

That's exactly what worries me. My voice drops. 'You don't think it's all a bit …' I cringe. 'Nerdy?'

Briana goes to speak, but Erin beats her to it. 'Why would you think that?'

'I don't know,' I say. 'The *debating team* …' What's to explain?

Erin's not the sort of person who would get this. I mean, she chose Hero Quest as her speech topic. She'd hardly even blink if anyone called her a nerd. She's kind of immune to it being an insult.

It's Briana who makes me feel better. 'Who cares if you're good at debating?' she says. 'I'd join the team if I could. That Jagath guy? He's really cute. And he's soooo smart, he'll probably be a doctor or something one day.'

'So?' says Erin.

'So, maybe this will be the start of something serious and Phoebs will end up marrying him.'

I'm laughing now, but Erin is all fired up. 'Briana!' she says. 'Maybe Phoebe's the one who'll be a doctor!'

'Hang on.' I laugh. 'I haven't even joined the team yet.'

'Well, you should,' says Erin. 'You'll be great.'

'And you'll get to drool over Jagath!' grins Briana.

'Yeah.' I shrug my shoulders as if it's no big deal, but I'm sure I'm blushing. It's not just that Jagath's gorgeous, he's really nice too.

Now I just have to talk Dad into letting me go to the meeting.

Chapter Three

That night, like every night since Mum's been away, Dad switches on the TV and we all watch with our dinner plates resting on our laps. Steph stabs a huge leaf of lettuce and bites at the wobbly end.

'Use a knife, Stephanie,' Dad says, as Steph does a drawn-out, dramatic sigh. Then he tells her sternly in Greek to sit at the table if she can't manage in here.

Steph rolls her eyes, folds the leaf into three and crams it on her fork. The ABC News starts, but Steph doesn't seem to notice. She shoves the whole leaf into her mouth and asks, chewing, 'When Mum comes back, will we have to eat at the table again?'

'Yes,' Dad says to the statue of the Virgin Mary on a shelf above our TV.

Steph's eyes track over to me, and we share a grin. Less than two weeks … But we know better than to keep talking during the news.

The first segment is about a tomato-canning factory closing down and shows people leaving on their last day. Dad shakes his head. A slow sigh.

Watching the news with Dad is like barracking for your favourite team. Police and firefighters get good comments. Politicians usually get sighs and abuse. Unless they have a Greek surname – all things Greek get bonus points.

They move through more stories: a famous murder trial, then a hurricane warning in Indonesia. Next up is a story about wild berries that are meant to lower your blood pressure. The medical expert they're interviewing is Indian, I think. He has a really strong accent.

The doctor's only said a few words when Dad shakes his head. 'And they expect us to take his word for it?'

'Why not?' asks Steph.

'Eh.' Dad grunts at the screen with his mouth turned down, but he doesn't answer.

Steph's eyes move back to the news and I see her taking in the doctor's dark skin, frowning slightly.

The doctor has the same complexion as Jagath. I start daydreaming about Jagath's broad chest until the sports presenter takes over. At our place that's as good as turning the TV off.

'How was the speech today?' Dad asks, before taking a bite of pastitsio.

'All right.' I place my cutlery on my plate. 'Once I got started it was fine.' I check Dad hasn't been distracted by the TV. He nods, so I keep going. 'At the end, Mr Mendes called me up and said I did really well. Like …' I take a breath. 'Top of the class.'

There's a pause as Dad takes it in, surprised but clearly pleased. 'Well … what do you know? *Syncharitiria!*'

Pride glows at the centre of my chest. At home I can talk about it without sounding like I'm bragging.

'Yeah, so this guy on the debating team,' I continue, 'he

even asked me to check out the next meeting because, you know, I was okay at speaking. But it's after school, so …'

Dad frowns. 'What day?'

'Um …' I make an act of thinking, even though I know exactly. 'Wednesday.'

'So …' He stares at the rug for a few seconds before his eyes lift. 'I'll finish early and pick up Steph.'

Really? I'm suddenly so excited I feel like jumping around and doing cartwheels. But how uncool is that? So I just say, 'Thanks, Dad.'

When the final bell goes on Wednesday, I grab my backpack and join the flow of traffic along the breezeway. It feels unnatural to peel off towards the library instead of heading out the school gates.

I wonder if Jagath singled me out just because he liked my speech. Or did he notice a bit more about me?

The library is totally abandoned, which is fine with me. Hanging out in the library after school is not a great look.

A door at the far side of the library stands open. I double-check the 'Study Room 3A' sign stuck on the front and stick my head through the doorway.

Jagath's head lifts and he cocks an eyebrow. 'Hey, Phoebe.'

Butterflies flit in my chest. His smile is even cuter than I remember.

Beside him, Zara nods distractedly while I find a seat opposite them. Maybe I've read this wrong. For all I know, something's already going on between Zara and Jagath. Zara's on my radar already because she's one of those all-rounders who blitzes everything. She's always being called up at assembly for awards, like Jagath. She's sporty too, and in the school band. I feel exhausted just looking at her.

'So, Phoebe, you're up for the interschool debate?' Zara asks, straight out. 'We don't have time to waste. It's a week from tomorrow.'

I wasn't expecting that. I shift in my seat. 'Well, I don't really know.' My voice is quieter than I'd like.

Mr Mendes pokes his head through the doorway. 'Great. You're all here.' He nods my way. 'Nice to see you,

Phoebe. I'll be in the next room if you need me, but I thought I'd leave you to discuss the topic yourselves, okay? I want you to take control of your own preparation.'

Jagath flips a page on his notepad. 'Fine by me.'

'Phoebe, I know you haven't done this before, but just see how you go today,' says Mr Mendes. 'I'm sure you'll be a real asset to the team.'

I nod. An interschool debate sounds terrifying. But Jagath is smiling at me, and Mr Mendes has already disappeared.

'Right.' Zara pulls a blank page from her folder. 'So. I'm thinking that I'll be first speaker, we can put Phoebe as second, and you can handle the rebuttal, Jagath, as third.' Zara turns from him to me. 'Okay?'

'Sure.' No way I'm disagreeing with Zara. Way to make life harder.

'So,' Zara says again. 'We're arguing for the affirmative. The topic is: That uniforms should be compulsory in schools.' With neat, rounded handwriting, she prints this at the top of her page.

'We're lucky,' says Jagath. 'We'll have consensus on our

side. I say we start with the obvious: uniforms keep us all on the same level, they disguise the rich–poor divide.'

Busily, they both begin to write. I just sit, thinking about the topic. Being forced to wear a uniform? I know all about that.

They're both writing down notes about the rich–poor divide when I say, 'Though that's really just spin they want you to believe.' Both pens hover and two faces tilt up at me. 'I mean, we all know who the rich kids are, uniform or no uniform. Have you seen the cars some of the parents drive?'

Jagath starts scribbling madly at the bottom of his page. 'I'll have to think up a rebuttal against that, just in case,' he mumbles.

I glance at Zara, worried that she'll think I'm being difficult, but she seems genuinely interested. She spreads her hands, palms open. 'I guess it's about brands,' she says slowly. 'No one's walking around with Nike this or Country Road that …'

'Yeah.' My mind races. 'But you can flip it the other way, and say that uniforms are about branding too. Like …

the school's branding. Uniforms help the school promote itself to the outside world. You could say they're *all* about class, and the rich–poor divide. I mean, some schools are really posh. And what about Kilmore High? You have to be super smart to get in there. Or really rich.'

Zara's shoulders actually slump as she turns to Jagath.

His cheeks bulge in a broad grin. 'What did I tell you?'

Head to one side, I check him out all over again. What *did* he tell her?

'Yeah …' Zara mumbles. 'Impressive.' She turns back to me and I'm glad that she doesn't seem annoyed, just intrigued. 'So what's our argument then?'

'That a school marketing itself is a good thing?' Jagath suggests.

'Or we could push it further and say that all schools should have exactly the same uniform, so that you can't tell the rich schools from the poor …' Zara says quietly.

'… or government schools from the private ones,' Jagath continues as they both start writing madly again.

'But if every school had the same uniform, and you couldn't tell which school anyone went to, what would be the point of wearing a uniform at all?' I say and grimace at the idea of a whole country of uniform-robot students.

No-one speaks for a few seconds. Zara and Jagath are both frozen with their pens in their hands.

'Phoebe, you're not actually helping!' Jagath says at last.

My eyes move from one face to the other. 'Sorry.'

'No, no … it's good to thrash out a topic,' Zara says, smiling encouragingly. 'We'll be supremely prepared for the opposition's arguments …' She drifts off and glances at her watch. 'But we'll have to sort out soon what we're going to say.'

'All right. Well, a uniform helps to identify kids from each school. And whatever you do while wearing it reflects on the school.' I nod decisively and pick up my pen.

Two seconds later I cross out everything I've written down. All I can think of is Mr Chiu whipping us into line, forcing everyone to pull up their socks and wipe off make-up. Uniforms may represent a school, but is that a good thing? Whatever happened to freedom of expression? Individuality?

Zara and Jagath are writing down all kinds of notes.

It feels as if I've been transported to the planet of high achievers. I tap my pen on my messy notepad. 'So, are you guys saying that you agree? You think it's a good thing to represent a group, and not be individuals?'

'I don't know,' Zara says without looking up. 'It's not as if we have a say, anyway.'

Jagath puts down his pen. 'This isn't about what we believe. It's about making a convincing argument …'

'… and winning the debate,' Zara adds.

'Okay?' Jagath asks. His dark eyes stay on me as he waits for my response.

'Yeah,' I say slowly, 'I guess.' But I don't add much to the discussion after that. Maybe it was a mistake, coming this afternoon.

How are you meant to argue for something you'd rather argue against?

At the end of the meeting, Mr Mendes hands out a permission slip for each of us to bring to school, and a registration form to bring on the day. 'And you'll have to organise a lift to the debate next Thursday. My car is already full with the senior team. Will that be okay?'

'Sure.' Zara grabs her forms and heads off for band practice.

I read through the pages. Am I really going to sign up for this?

When I look up, Mr Mendes is watching me. 'So, Phoebe, how was your first meeting?' When I hesitate, his forehead crinkles. 'What's wrong?'

A deep breath. I glance at Jagath, who's zipping up his backpack.

'Well. It's just …' I make a scrunched-up, apologetic sort of face. 'I'm not sure I really fit the team.' I pause as they look at me. I decide to come right out and say it: 'To be honest I'd rather argue for the opposite side. That we shouldn't have to wear uniforms at school. I have heaps to say about that … and there doesn't seem any point arguing for a side that I don't agree with.'

Jagath frowns. Is he disappointed? He's so hard to read.

'I see.' Mr Mendes pauses, but there's a sparkle in his

eyes. It's almost as if he's pleased with what I just said. 'A good debater can argue for either side,' he says carefully. 'That's the whole point of a debate. You'd be surprised how differently you see an issue once you understand it from both perspectives.'

'Sure, but …' I lift my shoulders and let them drop. 'I already know both sides of this topic. And I know which one I'm on.'

'Think of it this way,' Jagath says. 'Did you see the news last night? That guy who's charged with murder but keeps saying he's innocent. He deserves to explain his side, doesn't he?'

'Yes, of course,' I say quickly. 'Innocent until proven guilty.'

'Exactly,' says Mr Mendes. 'And just as every criminal case deserves its day in court, every topic in a debate also deserves due consideration.'

I rub my forehead, playing with the idea of actually trying to come up with a decent argument. They make it seem so worthwhile. 'That uniforms should be compulsory in schools …' I say quietly.

Mr Mendes nods. 'Anyway, what do you have to lose?' he says after a while. 'You might even change your mind about uniforms.'

'I seriously doubt that.'

Jagath's eyebrows go up. 'So?'

'Okay, count me in,' I nod. 'I'm on the team.'

'Great. I'm pleased to hear that.' Mr Mendes says. Then Jagath breaks into a broad grin, and I'm suddenly even more glad I've said yes.

Jagath's so cute when he smiles.

Chapter
Four

Once we've packed up at the end of the meeting, Jagath and I head to the front of the school. It feels sort of *tempting* being alone with him. Him and me. Me and him.

We cut through the office without speaking. As we make our way out the main doors, Jagath glances at me then away. I smooth a hand over my hair.

We're passing the front noticeboard when he turns to me. 'So we're meeting again at my place on Saturday, okay? Try to think up some arguments by then.'

'Okay.' I'm searching for something more to say, but nothing comes.

'Arguments for our side, I mean,' Jagath teases.

'Oh … really?' I play dumb and then let out a laugh.

We come to a stop beside the school gate. Jagath drops his bag while I check up the road. No sign of Dad. For the next few minutes we just stand there, checking the passing cars. Every now and then I glance sideways at Jagath, wondering what he's thinking.

The silence is beginning to feel weird, so I shift my backpack and glance at him for about the fourteenth time. 'So, is your family Indian?' I ask, by way of conversation.

He looks at me strangely. 'Sri Lankan. Why?'

Oh no, now I've really stuffed up. 'Just wondering,' I say quickly. 'Sorry. I didn't mean to be rude.'

Jagath breaks into an amused grin. 'Don't stress. I was two when we moved here, so I count myself more Australian than anything else.'

I match his grin. 'Yeah, I know what you mean. My dad's Greek, but I've never been there. I'm Australian too.'

A car turns the corner and we both pause to look.

'Do you want to go to Greece?' Jagath asks once the car passes. 'One day?'

'Sure,' I say, and lean against the fence. 'I'd love to see the Acropolis and the village where Dad's from. What about you?'

Jagath drops his head to one side. 'Do I want to see the village where your dad's from?'

'No, I meant do you want to go to Sri Lanka?' I say, but then he breaks into another grin and I realise he was teasing me.

'I've been a couple of times. We have relatives over there. But I want to see all over Asia. Borneo especially.'

The next few minutes disappear with talk about rainforests being cut down and species dying out. Turns out Jagath's really easy to talk to. Each time I speak, he looks as if he really wants to hear what I have to say. I've never met a guy who listens the way he does.

We're leaning over his phone, our heads almost touching as we add up how much it would cost for a trip to Borneo, when I hear my name.

'Phoebe!' Something in the tone of Dad's voice makes me step back and I turn to see him striding towards us. When I glance at Jagath it suddenly feels weird, as if

I've been caught doing something I shouldn't. I'd totally forgotten to check for the car.

'Sorry. Have to go,' I say.

Jagath nods. 'Catch you tomorrow?'

'Yeah.' I've already started towards Dad, so I turn back and shoot him a smile. 'See you then.'

Dad reaches me in a few seconds, and peers at Jagath. Then he starts straight into a stream of Greek about how he had to leave Steph in the car.

'Sorry, I didn't see you drive up,' I say when I finally get a chance to speak. We cross the road, stopping halfway on the median strip for a couple of cars.

Once we reach the other side, I turn to Dad and grin. 'So guess what? I'm on the team! The schedule's really tight. I'm meant to plan my speech before we meet this weekend.'

Dad and I walk around a parked car, and then meet up on the other side. 'And I'll need a lift on the actual day,' I say carefully.

He nods, and I expect him to say something about taking time off work, but then Dad asks, 'What was going on with that Indian kid?'

'Oh, that's Jagath,' I say, testing the way his name comes out. Think I nailed it this time. 'He's on the team and is really smart. Funny too …' I bite my lip. 'He's actually Sri Lankan.'

'*Ti mou les*,' Dad says under his breath.

I'm not even sure what that means. Something like 'unbelievable', I think.

Dad starts muttering to himself about the souvlaki joint that used to be on the corner, and how they're turning that into an Indian restaurant now too. I'm not really sure what this has to do with anything. But I don't say that. Dad's attitude to Greek food is sort of the way I feel about make-up. It's how we show the world who we are.

We reach the car and Dad bips the lock. Steph's sitting in the front, head poking up, pretending to drive with her hands on the steering wheel. While Dad tells her off, I slip into my seat.

'Hi, Steph,' I call over my shoulder.

'Why can't I sit in the front?' She's panting from having climbed into the back.

I shift around so I can see her properly. 'Because it's my turn.'

Steph crosses her arms and pouts.

The engine whirrs to life as Dad twists the key. I settle in and click my belt. Just three days until the next debate meeting. I have to come up with a decent argument before then.

Straight after dinner, I get stuck into research for the debate.

There's loads of stuff online and the main argument seems to be that uniforms stop people standing out as advantaged or disadvantaged. A couple of the articles say wearing a uniform stops people getting distracted by provocative clothing. That's totally not true. It's possible to lose an entire period because you're in the same class as a guy you're crushing on, uniform or no uniform. Speaking from experience.

And then there's the argument that uniforms 'instil discipline'. If you turn up at school in a uniform, then you turn up expecting to work. Which, again, is totally not true. Still speaking from experience.

I've been working for ten minutes when my mind wanders, just for a moment. I realise I haven't checked *Glamour Girl* online for nearly twenty-four hours. Or Briana might be up for a chat. Or maybe I could try that new nail polish I bought …

Normally I would have found something better to do about nine minutes ago. But tonight, I don't. I'm part of the debating team now. I can actually feel Jagath hovering on one shoulder like some sort of gorgeous ghost, expecting me to come up with something half decent. Counting on me, really.

So, this time, I keep searching.

I have twelve million results at my fingertips. Twelve million. So you'd think that someone would have come up with an argument I can agree with.

Problem is, the more I search, the more I find, well … more of the same. Some of the articles even use the same phrasing as others I've already read, and it takes me only a few more minutes to work out what's been going on.

All around the world, kids have been getting this same question as a debate topic, or essay topic, or whatever. And what's the first thing they do? Exactly what I'm doing now. They jump online, scroll down all the articles they can find on the topic, pick a few that seem fair enough, and then use those arguments to make notes. The same ideas. The same argument. Over and over. Twelve million times.

I keep searching, honestly I do, but now it's with a growing sense of dread. Because I really need to have something to contribute this weekend, or I'll look like an idiot in front of Zara and Jagath.

Thinking of Jagath reminds me of the stuff we talked about while we were waiting to be picked up. I find myself googling Sri Lanka, which is way more interesting than compulsory uniforms. All these images come up of gorgeous beaches, tropical rainforests and cinnamon crops, crumbling temples and ancient buildings. I start reading about the country's cultures and religions. That takes me to a whole pile of new info about some civil war that went on for twenty-six years. It's all pretty incredible.

But by the time I have to go to bed, I've gone flat about the whole debate. I was actually trying my best and I still don't have any decent arguments.

I could just use the same arguments as the ones online, I guess. But it's hard to feel inspired about that.

Just because everyone says the same thing over and over doesn't make it true.

I'm cramming my backpack into my locker the next morning when Jagath appears beside me.

'How's your debate prep going?'

I swing my locker door shut. 'S'okay.' There's no way I'm admitting to Jagath that I'm having trouble. Better to keep my mouth shut until I come up with a dazzling argument and totally blow him away …

Jagath stands there as if expecting me to say more, and there's this full-on moment where we just look into each other's eyes. You can totally tell how smart he is, I decide, from the way he looks at you so carefully. I get this feeling that he's going to say something …

'Sure you don't want to do a run-through before we meet next?' he says. 'It's good to practise.'

That sure wasn't the moment I was hoping for. 'I'll be okay.' I've got nothing to run through anyway.

'Is Saturday arvo still good for you?' Jagath holds out a blue sticky note with an address and phone number. 'Here's my address.'

'Thanks.' I stick the note inside my folder and take a deep breath. 'I'll get Dad to drop me off after seeing Mum –'

Jagath's face goes serious. 'How's she doing?'

'Good, actually. She's due home a week from Saturday.' We head towards our next class. I hug my books to my chest.

'Bet you miss her,' he says quietly.

I drop my chin. Yeah, I do. A group of people from the drama group pass us in a rush, gushing about auditions for the school play.

There's more I could say about Mum, but I don't. She's out of the worst, but it's still awful for other reasons. We speak on the phone most nights, but it's not the same. I don't want to say anything remotely negative or worry her. She already feels so distant.

We're almost at the demountables now. It's always quieter at this end of the school. First up is homeroom, but we're in different groups. When we reach my classroom, I pause at the bottom of the steps and turn to face Jagath. I may not have any arguments for the debate yet, but I can start a different brainiac topic.

'So, I read something about a civil war,' I say casually. 'In Sri Lanka.'

Just slightly, Jagath frowns. 'You hadn't heard about that?'

'Oh, yeah ... of course,' I say, though the honest answer is 'not at all'. I guess I never really tune in to the war stories on the news.

'Is that ...' I begin, and then want to take it back. Is it rude to ask someone about their country's war? What if someone in his family was killed or something else terrible happened?

'Is that ... why we moved to Australia?' Jagath finishes for me, and I'm glad he's not upset. He sighs. 'Well, yeah, it was a factor, but we moved to be close to family. My uncle's the head chef at the Brighton Hotel. You know it?' I nod, and Jagath keeps going. 'He needed more staff, so he asked Dad. Sri Lankan curries are pretty awesome.'

'Yeah?' My family doesn't really eat curry. Probably because Dad loves Greek food so much.

Jagath checks his watch. 'Anyway, don't want to be late. See you later?'

'Yep, see you.' I watch as he disappears down the path. Smart, cute, and right on time.

During homeroom, Erin, Briana and I find our usual spots up the back. We sit in a row leaning our chairs against the wall so we can swing our legs.

Other people are filtering in, finding places in front of us. 'So … what else do you guys know about Jagath?' I keep my voice low.

'Other than the fact he's cute?' Briana says. 'Well, sort of quiet.' She looks over at me. Her legs stop mid-swing and she turns to me as it sinks in. 'Jagath?'

It's one thing to agree that some guy's a hottie, but something else to admit you really like him. Glad he's not in the same homeroom as us. I check to see if anyone else is listening and make a shy sort of shrug.

Ms Schilling calls out the first name on the roll and we all shrink a little lower, out of sight. She calls my name and I yell, 'Here!' before shrinking again.

'Has he ever been out with anyone, do you know?' I ask quietly.

None of the other guys I've had crushes on have been like him. Smart but sort of humble at the same time. And strangely mysterious …

'Nope,' says Briana.

'No idea,' whispers Erin, and then loud for Mrs Schilling: 'Here!'

Briana breaks into a grin and nudges me. 'This is so cute. I was just mucking around about you marrying him. I never would've picked you falling for him for real.'

'Why not?'

There's a pause. Then Ms Schilling keeps calling names.

'He just seems really serious about school,' Erin whispers.

'I can be serious about school.' I wasn't meaning it as a joke but they both crack up, smothering the sound behind hands. 'What? I'm on the debating team, aren't I?' But I end up joining in.

It's okay. They're right. Who am I kidding? Jagath's not the sort of guy to fall for someone like me. He doesn't seem to have picked up the same vibe between us. He's probably madly in love already with some girl who's about to crack the secret to clean energy. Someone who's really smart.

I can't even get my head around any good reason why we're stuck with compulsory uniforms.

Chapter Five

'When Mum comes home,' Steph calls over the hum of the car engine, 'will you have to sit in the back seat with me?'

'Of course.' I twist around so I can see her.

She crosses her arms. 'Good.'

The trip to Aunty Celia's house always seems to take forever. Especially once Steph gets bored and starts kicking the back of my seat. Thud. Like just now.

'Stop it!' I yell for the millionth time.

'Not doing anything,' Steph calls, but there's victory in her voice.

Thud. Just ignore it. 'So, we'll have to leave at, maybe two-thirty so I can get to the meeting?'

Dad makes this 'eh' sound that's not much more than a grunt, the same answer he gave when I told him about it last night. Slowly he inhales. 'Whose house?'

'Jagath's,' I say. 'You know, the guy who was waiting with me on Wednesday night?'

No response. It takes me a while to find the sticky note in my backpack, rocking with the car as I rifle around. I pull it out. 'It's at fifty-three Salisbury Court, Hepburn,' I read slowly.

Another grunt.

Another thud. This is getting on my nerves. I swivel fast, trying to catch her out. 'Stop it already!'

'Not doing anything.' Steph pokes out her tongue and I shoot back a glare.

Dad flicks the indicator. 'I've been thinking,' he says slowly in Greek, 'maybe they have a debating team at the Hellenic school. And I think there's a youth group at the Orthodox Church.'

I make a face. 'What does that have to do with anything?'

'You could practise your Greek,' Dad says and shrugs. 'Who knows? You might make a few friends.' He glances over at me, smiling as if we're sharing a dad–daughter moment.

I face straight ahead. 'I already have friends.'

'It hasn't been easy for you, though, has it, settling in at McEwan College? Maybe if you met other Greek kids, people more like us …'

More like us? This whole conversation is getting on my nerves. If Zara had been waiting with me on Wednesday, would Dad be going on about Greek school now?

Another thud.

'How about this?' My voice rises over the noise of the car. 'If you're so keen to hang out with a bunch of Greeks, why don't *you* sign up for wog school?'

Dad's forehead creases, not impressed. 'What did you call it?'

'Nothing,' I say quietly. Everyone calls it that, even the Greek kids. But you can't say it in front of Dad.

'Be-have your-self,' he says, enunciating each syllable to make his point. A pause. Then it all comes out in a stream of Greek: He has a lot on his plate at the moment. Work is crazy. Mum's still not home. If I want a lift to the meeting, then I have to show some respect. 'Okay?'

When I don't say anything, he asks again: 'Okay?'

A sigh. 'Okay.'

Dad pulls up outside Aunty Celia's and checks the clock. 'We'll leave here at a quarter to three,' he announces, though he's calmer now.

Arms crossed, I follow behind Steph as she charges up the path. The door opens just as Steph reaches the porch. She's through in a flash and Celia's left in a trail of wind.

'Hello, Stephanie!' Celia calls over her shoulder. A smile for me. 'Hi, Phoebe.'

'How is she?' We hug hello and I get the same feeling I always have around Celia. She's like Mum, but not. Sort of how Mum might seem to people who don't know her.

'Better.' She pulls away, nodding. 'Much, much better.'

Dad's on the porch by now, so I don't hang around, but continue down the hall.

To Mum. Just the sight of her gives me this pang in the chest. She's so small and thin in Celia's flowery armchair.

Steph's already in Position A, of course, perched on Mum's lap.

I peck her cheek and then have to wait while Steph goes on about all her little-big things. Sore finger. A spider's web in the car. The bruise on her banana. I wait, trying to be patient.

Celia shares out biscuits with coffee. There's lemonade for me and Steph.

About a hundred hours later, Steph makes it to the end of her news and Mum's eyes track across to me. 'Phoebe? How are you?'

'Okay.' I do my best to find a smile. It's never enough, seeing her like this, with Celia hovering and Dad waiting for his turn.

We chat about my friends and I ask how she's feeling. Mum says she's much better, thanks, same as always. I tell her everything's going well at school, but I don't say anything about my speech. If I did, she'd want to know the topic, and I couldn't admit that to her. I don't want to make her feel guilty or anything.

'And how's Steph at night?' Mum asks at one point.

Automatically, I glance out the back door, where Steph's trying to get some action out of Celia's lazy labrador.

'Oh, she's fine,' I answer breezily.

That's just the way I talk to Mum these days, toning everything down so she won't worry. Like Steph's nightmares, for instance. I haven't told Mum about them. She knows Steph's been sleeping in my room, but I haven't told her exactly why. So many things have happened that she knows nothing about.

Like, Steph keeps having nightmares.

Like, I told the whole class how sick you were, and people really listened.

Like, Dad decided we're all moving to Greece because this cute guy at school is freaking him out.

I reach out to push the bell at Jagath's place, then flick my hair and straighten my top. It feels as if I'm standing on stage, waiting for a curtain to part.

I notice a mountain bike resting against the porch rail,

and a row of shoes neatly lined up by the door. Dad's car is still idling at the kerb. He's waiting, I guess, to make sure I'm at the right place.

The door opens and Jagath's suddenly standing in front of me. 'Hi,' he says. 'Come in.'

'Sorry I'm late.' I cringe. It's 3.08. Could be worse.

'No problem.' He sees Dad's car at the kerb and motions behind me. 'Oh … do they want to come in? They're more than welcome.'

As if in response, Dad pulls away and disappears down the road. I shrug and make this face that's meant to mean *never mind.*

Inside, Jagath's eyes fix onto mine, but it's not at all awkward. It's as if we're somehow talking without using words.

Made it at last …

I'm glad you're here.

Jagath breathes in. 'Come through,' he says and gestures along the hall.

We reach the kitchen and Jagath introduces me to his mum. She's short and has the same round cheeks as him.

She's wearing the most beautiful blue cotton wrap with white trimming.

'Hello,' she says with a shy nod. She gazes past me expectantly, looking for a parent, I guess, and I suddenly feel rude not to have brought Dad in to meet her.

'My little sister …' I point over my shoulder. 'Dad didn't want to leave her waiting in the car.'

'Oh.' Her hands lift to her face. 'Should I come out?'

'No, no. He's already gone.' I shake my head quickly, her awkwardness somehow making it worse.

'Don't stress, Mum,' Jagath says from the other side of the room. He jerks his head for me to follow.

We end up in the living room, and Zara glances up from a table near the window. 'Heeey!' she says warmly. 'You're here!'

'Sorry I'm late.' I head over to sit next to her. It's sparsely furnished in here, way less clutter than my place, and other than a serene-looking Buddha statue sitting cross-legged on the mantelpiece it could be anyone's home.

'So. We forgot to define the topic when we met last time,' Zara says once we're all sorted. 'But I think it's pretty straightforward. Compulsory just means everyone has to wear them.'

I'm starting to see how she excels in so many different things: band, netball, school and debate team. She gets on with it. No messing around googling stuff she's not working on.

'And we also need to work out some sort of case statement,' Zara says.

I'm still settling into my chair. 'Some sort of what?'

'A sentence or a phrase that sums up our argument,' she says simply. 'And we all say it to emphasise the point, you know?'

For a while we say nothing. 'Uniforms are useful?' Jagath asks, then shakes his head.

'Hey, I like the way you used two U's,' I say encouragingly.

'Anyway …' Zara checks her watch. 'Have a think and let me know if you come up with any other ideas.' She pulls out a sheet of paper. 'Here's a template for you to use when you're writing your speech.'

'Template?' My eyes scan down.

'Yeah,' Zara says. 'Use that when you're working out the details of your speech. You have to say those bits in bold …'

As she points, I read out the first line: 'Good afternoon chairman, members of the audience. The topic for our debate is …'

'Exactly, and then you fill in the blanks according to our argument. Like, the topic for our debate is that uniforms should be compulsory, right?'

While Zara's talking, I read the rest of the bold parts. We, the affirmative/negative team, believe that this statement is true/false.

And then it keeps going:

The opposition speaker has tried to tell you …

This is wrong because …

Blah.

It's the uniform-version of public speaking. First, everyone is forced to dress the same. Now everyone's talking the same?

'But can't we, you know, say it in our own words?' I ask.

'Yeah, sure. But within that basic structure,' Zara says. 'Okay?' As if it's the easiest thing in the world.

Except I'm not as good as she is when it comes to following rules. Once again, I get the *pfft* feeling in my brain. The sound of inspiration choking to death.

Zara spends a bit of time going over things I need to do in my speech, like refuting arguments and repeating our case statement. She talks about all the things the adjudicator will mark us on. Jagath warns me about a bell they ring when it's a good idea to start summarising, and the second bell, a double: the one to worry about.

Jagath's mum brings in a plate of this amazing roti bread and some dips while we're working. The bread's so light and warm that it just seems to melt in my mouth. It's completely yum.

We drift off topic for a while then, tearing off pieces of roti and talking about the other schools in the competition.

It's only when the plate is empty that we start working again. Zara stands at the end of the table and runs through her opening speech. She keeps saying stuff like *I'll fix up that part* and *I'm still working on this bit*. But she hardly needs to. It's really good. Like *really* good. Way better than mine's going to be.

For one thing, I'm not even sure what to say.

I'm madly trying to remember the arguments I found online when the doorbell rings.

Zara checks her watch. 'Sorry, team.' She slips her cue cards into a pocket in her backpack. 'Have to go. Netball fundraiser.'

'Really?' I raise my eyebrows, but inside I'm thinking, *phew*. Saved by the over-achiever.

Jagath disappears to see Zara out and I check my watch. Fifteen more minutes before Dad's due to pick me up. Jagath comes back and takes the seat that Zara was just in. Beside me.

'So, how's your argument coming along?' He leans an elbow on the table, head in his hand.

It gives me a little shiver inside. Him and me. Me and him. But I have to stop myself thinking this way. Any interest here is a one-way street.

I breathe in. Get a grip. 'Not too bad,' I say. 'I saw some ideas online.' Somehow I find a bit of crumpled paper with my notes and smooth it flat. 'Uniforms stop you getting distracted by provocative clothing …' I glance up.

Jagath nods.

I clear my throat. Check my notes. 'Wearing a uniform puts you in the frame of mind to work …'

Again I glance up to find him watching me closely, utterly locked on to what I'm saying.

I place my paper on the table. Sinking a little. The more time I spend around Jagath, the more I want to do a good job. Not just because he's cute. But because his standards are so high when it comes to work like this. Zara's too.

'To be honest?' I sigh. 'Most of the stuff online is just boring. More of the same, you know? None of the arguments were all that impressive, if you ask me.' I check his expression. 'I haven't found anything that convinces me uniforms are a good idea.'

Jagath shrugs. 'Don't worry about the stuff online. Come up with your own ideas.' As if that's the easiest thing in the world. 'You were really good on the fly at our team meeting. Anyone can research, but not many people can come up with their own argument.'

I can't help a little grin at that. 'Well … thanks.' But

now I'm right back where I started. All my own ideas are for the opposite side.

'Something else I find that helps,' Jagath says, leaning forward. 'Try putting yourself in their shoes. Like, someone who might agree with your argument. It's something my mum goes on about, from Buddhism. To see people as they truly are, you need to be able to understand their point of view.'

But who would agree with the idea of compulsory uniforms? 'Do you?' I ask casually. 'Agree with compulsory uniforms?'

'Well …' He glances down at his T-shirt. Faded blue with a black design. Carelessly casual. 'I'm not too fussed about fashion. Let's just say I can see it both ways.'

'Yeah, okay.' But this has me thinking. I'm about to ask Jagath if he knows what Zara would say when my phone chimes. It's Dad.

Out front.

For a few seconds, I just stare at the text. What's wrong with him? Why didn't he ring the doorbell like a normal person? Slowly, my eyes lift. 'That's my ride.'

'I'll walk you out.'

We reach the front porch and there's Dad's car, the engine running. For some reason, the sight of it makes my muscles tense. Mum would never have done this.

I swivel to face Jagath. 'Thanks for having me. See you on Monday.'

Jagath smiles. 'See ya.'

Steph's in the front, but I don't miss a beat, slipping into the back and checking out my window, just in time to see the front door close.

Dad finds my reflection in the rear-view mirror. 'How was it?'

'Fine.'

He glances my way again but I pretend I don't notice.

All the way home I'm quiet, thinking about Jagath. He's so easy to talk to; I'm glad I came clean. His advice is exactly the help I need. The whole trip home, I mull it over in my mind. Who would agree that uniforms should be compulsory? Erin?

No.

Mr Cartwright? Probably.

We're pulling into the driveway when it hits me.

Mr Chiu. Of course! Why didn't I think of him sooner? I just have to get inside his crazy, robotic mind. Then I'll have the debate argument of the century.

Chapter Six

Operation Communicate With The Enemy begins early on Monday morning.

I'm prepared for the mission: uniform worn exactly to regulation, giving me that perfect sack-of-potatoes look that's so in this season. I don't even sneak into the toilets for my daily magic tricks. If I'm going into enemy territory, I'll need to dress the way he expects me to, as if I'm on his side.

I arrive well before the buses so there's less chance that anyone will see me – but I still have a sense of urgency about getting this done. I stay close to buildings – around A block, past the demountables and then a quick scan of the oval.

Problem is, with no-one here Mr Chiu has no need for uniform reconnaissance. If I'm going to get this finished quickly, I have to enter enemy headquarters. The vice-principal's office.

Through one of the internal windows, I'm able to see Mr Chiu before he sees me. He's busy typing, back straight as a pole.

I pull a notebook and pen out of my bag before tapping on his door. Not because I'm planning to take notes or anything, but because teachers like Mr Chiu love stuff like that.

'Yes!' barks Mr Chiu as soon as I knock. I push the door open, and his head jerks up. He's wearing a shirt and tie. A pinstripe jacket hangs over his chair. Nice. 'Yes?' he says again, softer this time.

'Hi, Mr Chiu, I'm Phoebe Cholas. Do you have a minute?' With my head up and shoulders back, I step into the office. Show no fear. He can smell it, I'm sure.

Mr Chiu glances at the clock, then at a chair beside his desk. 'Take a seat.'

Neat as a pin, I slip into place, keeping my feet flat and my knees together in that awkward way they make you sit on photo day.

'I'm on the junior debating team,' I begin, 'and I was wondering if you'd be willing to share your thoughts on the topic? We're arguing that uniforms should be compulsory in schools.'

'Ah ...' A pause. Mr Chiu leans back and considers me for a moment. 'Well. Let me see.' He adjusts his position in the chair. Somehow his back ends up even straighter than before. 'A uniform is futile unless it's compulsory,' Mr Chiu says simply.

Wow. Straight out, that's a good argument. It definitely needs to be part of our definition at the start. No point having a uniform if only some people wear it.

I'm holding a pen and paper, aren't I? Might as well use them. I quickly scribble a note, so I remember to tell Zara.

'And then there are reasons of discipline, focus,' continues Mr Chiu briskly, 'projecting an image of success.'

As he speaks, my eyes scan the objects in the room, trying to get a sense of what it's like to be Mr Chiu. Put myself in his shoes …

A series of photos line the back wall. Most of them show Mr Chiu with a bunch of students. Prefects, probably. They're all standing in groups, grinning with their heads held high. All in uniform, of course. Mr Chiu stands with the same straight back among them all. In one, he's actually laughing.

I hold my pen ready. 'So, it's about image then?'

'Of course, but it's more than that …' Mr Chiu pauses and a faint smile flickers. 'Want to know why I care so much about uniforms?'

I nod, so he leans back in his chair.

'Every morning when I walk around the school grounds, I see students arriving from all over. But their uniforms give them a sense of community. Each student has a place here. Everyone belongs.'

My pen rests on the paper, but it hasn't formed any letters. I just stare at Mr Chiu.

Everyone belongs … The way he's talking, it's almost

making me proud to be wearing our school uniform. Almost.

He crosses his legs, and takes a few seconds to settle again. 'You could call it the dress code of our school family.'

As I think about my response, I cross my legs, matching his pose. 'Yes, but we'd still be a community if we were in free dress,' I test. 'You don't need to wear the same clothes in order to belong to the same school.'

'No,' Mr Chiu says. Slowly he nods, as if considering what I just said. 'But we would appear less of a community, don't you agree?'

I think this is what I was getting at, back in the library, when I said uniforms gave us an identity. But I hadn't expressed it this well. I was still thinking of it as being something forced on us, rather than something that brings us together. 'Yeah, I guess I do.'

'And you know as well as I do that appearance can have an impact, whether we like it or not.'

'Yes,' I say softly, but it's with a degree of shock. Because even though I knew he'd be all for compulsory uniforms, I actually agree with him. Not pretending to agree just for the debate, or trying to imagine I'm someone else. I agree with Mr Chiu on this. Go figure …

'Okay?' He glances at the clock.

'Yes, that's great.' I'm out of my seat and smiling. 'Thanks, sir.'

Mr Chiu stands too, his expression stern once again as he pulls his jacket around his shoulders.

My hand is reaching for the doorknob when Mr Chiu calls out behind me. 'And Phoebe? Good luck with the debate.'

My eyebrows go up.

'You clearly have a good grasp of the topic,' he adds. 'It's obvious that you understand the reasons for dressing appropriately.' A pause. 'You were smart enough to come in here without make-up on today,' he says with a smile.

Straight out of Mr Chiu's office, I stop to jot down notes. *Sense of community. Family.* People who break dress code and try to stand out as individuals: I guess to Mr Chiu they're saying that they don't want to belong.

I'm not entirely sure where I sit with the argument now. Am I on the fence, able to see both sides? Or do I think that both sides are sometimes right, depending on the situation?

It doesn't really matter what I think for now because I have a debate coming up and I'll be arguing that uniforms should be compulsory. Each side of an argument has a right to be heard. At least now I'll be able to argue for our case without feeling like a complete fraud.

Once I've finished jotting notes, I decide to search out Zara and tell her the slant that Mr Chiu gave us about uniforms being pointless unless they're compulsory, and the other stuff he said about community. I'm not sure where she hangs out before school, but I know the main haunts for people in our year. I start by heading down the slope to the basketball courts, checking beyond them and across the oval.

Most of the buses are here by now, all sorts of groups dotted around, catching up again after a weekend apart, smiling or cracking jokes when more people arrive. It's the same scene every day, really, but I can't help remembering how out of it all I felt when I was new.

Zara's nowhere near the oval so I head back up towards the canteen area. Larger crowds hang around the tables, and I have to scan each person to check if they're Zara or not. Maybe it would be easier to pick her in a crowd if we were wearing our own choice of clothes ...

I'm scanning the sea of faces when one stands out among the rest. A cute and familiar face.

Jagath reacts as soon as he sees me, breaking into a broad grin and stepping forward expectantly.

I wave subtly. 'Hey there.'

'Hey,' he says. 'You look kinda different.'

'Different ... how?' Then I realise what's going on. No make-up. He thinks I'm all pale and pasty, as if I'm sick.

'I don't know,' Jagath continues. 'Just different. Like you're happier or something.'

Different good? I smile. 'Really?' There's a weird pause when I think Jagath's about to say more, but then he glances away.

'So, guess who I just saw?' I ask. 'The Uniform Robot.'

'Who?' Jagath looks confused.

'I took your advice, right? About asking someone who would agree that uniforms should be compulsory?' He nods so I keep going. 'Mr Chiu was really helpful. He talked about uniforms bringing people together, showing how we all belong …'

'Maybe we could use that for our case statement,' says Jagath. He holds out his arms as if preparing for a huge announcement. 'Uniforms bring us together.' He waits for my response.

'Hey, I like that … except, we don't have the two U's anymore.' I'm sort of joking, but still … I thought the first one had a good ring to it.

'Uniforms are useful in bringing us together,' Jagath mumbles, then shakes his head.

'Uniforms bring us together usefully?' My nose scrunches. Bad.

We throw ideas around for a while, cracking up at our tongue twisters and other bad phrases.

After a while, Jagath goes serious. 'What about this? Uniforms unite us.'

'Three U's in a row!' I cheer. 'That's it! I really like it.'

We find Zara next, hanging out on the steps in front of C block. She likes our idea for a case statement straight away.

'Hey, I can totally use that,' she says, each nod increasing in speed. 'I can hang my whole argument off that one idea …'

I'm also nodding when I realise I can too. After seeing Mr Chiu and thinking about our case statement I can totally see our side of the debate. Already I can think of two clear arguments to use.

Right until the first bell goes we discuss the debate, brainstorming ideas and helping each other with our arguments. I can feel my brain firing in ways it never has before, and it's a complete buzz.

Chapter
Seven

I'm still buzzing at the start of recess, trying out phrases in my mind that I might be able to use. Better keep a lid on it, or someone will catch me muttering my speech to myself.

The guy who has the locker next to mine is already here so I put my head down and get on with my usual gear swap. As I close my door I brush a hand lightly over my forearm before clicking the lock. Already spiky gorilla hair has begun to grow back. I was so keen to see Mr Chiu that I didn't shave this morning.

It's only when I look up that I realise the guy's been watching. Our eyes meet and his cheeks turn a shade pinker, as if I caught him spying. I just smile vaguely and pretend I haven't noticed him looking at my gorilla arms, and he looks away.

Then I see he has a poster of a model on the inside of his locker door. She's in a bikini, but you can see her boobs bulging out of it. There's no hint of any hair out of place. In fact, there's no hint of hair at all on her body.

I've been staring at the poster for so long now that the guy glances back my way, and it's as if we're both thinking the same thing, but neither of us wants to admit it. As if we're both playing this strange sort of spot the difference. Model against Gorilla Girl.

My smile tries to wobble, but I don't give it permission. I just act as if I'm not remotely fussed and spin the other way. It's not until I'm further along the corridor that my steps increase in speed.

Erin's the only one at our bench when I get there. I slump down and sigh.

'You all right?' she asks.

'Sure.' But I'm not, exactly. Why do I have to be a gorilla? I'm probably even hairier than Locker Guy, and he's a *guy*. They're meant to be hairy and gross.

'Where's Briana?' I say, changing the subject.

'Volleyball tryouts.' Erin keeps watching me. 'Sure you're all right?'

'Yeah, it's … not as if I can do anything about it, anyway.'

'What?'

I shake my head. Erin's not the sort of person who would get something like this. 'You'll just tell me I'm being dumb.'

I'm expecting to leave it there, but Erin swivels so she's looking right at me, one leg tucked under her bum. 'Come on, try me.'

Even though Erin's not going to get it, I take a breath and tell her all about the model, and how I felt comparing myself to her.

Erin listens intently at first. Halfway through, her face scrunches the way she does when she thinks I'm insane. Here we go.

'You realise that in real life she doesn't look like that,' Erin says when I've finished. 'They would have fixed up her freckles and pimples and stuff in Photoshop.'

'Yeah, I know, but …' I lift my arm so Erin can see and rub a finger over the black spiky hairs. 'Look. I shaved two days ago, and now look at it …'

'Yeah, so …' Erin lifts a shoulder as if I'm being Captain Obvious. 'It's just your genes!'

'My stupid hairy genes.' I glare at my arm. I can almost *see* the hair growing.

When I look up again, Erin's still watching me with her mouth squashed to one side the way she does when she's fed up with talk about clothes or make-up. Before she can say it, I get in first. 'Yeah, all right. I know what you're going to say … it's who you are on the inside that counts.'

'Nope.' Erin shakes her head seriously. 'I wasn't going to say that at all. I was going to say that if you didn't have your Greek genes, you wouldn't have those big eyes or that shiny black hair,' she says simply. 'Look at this blonde fluff I have for hair.' She smiles. 'Everyone has things they don't like about themselves. Even models. Actually, especially models. They must be obsessed with the way they look. Every tiny imperfection would be scrutinised.'

True, I guess. But that doesn't stop me hating the gorilla within.

We're quiet for a bit, but I can tell she's frowning my way, biting her lip. Not annoyed, exactly. More like she's concerned.

'You don't need to stress about some poster, Phoebe,' Erin says after a while. 'You just need to enjoy the good parts of what you have. You have heaps of stuff going for you.' She gives me a friendly nudge with her shoulder. 'And you're really smart! Annoyingly smart.'

I definitely wasn't expecting her to say that.

'How else do you get away with doing, like, *zero* work, and still pass everything?' Erin's voice rises as she speaks, as if she's been thinking it for a while. 'I have to work really hard to get the marks I do. But you just coast through, hardly trying at all.'

'I do so work.' I half shrug. 'Well, some of the time. And my marks aren't exactly good.'

Erin swings back around so we're sitting side by side. 'I bet Briana would kill to have it half as easy as you do at school.'

We're quiet for a bit, but it doesn't seem weird. I think about Briana, who does try really hard, and just barely scrapes through with a pass. Erin's right. And even though I'm still desperate to shave, I'm glad I told Erin what happened.

Briana and Hamish are heading over when I feel another nudge from Erin.

'Let's make a deal,' she says quietly. 'Next time you see a picture of some model, and it makes you feel all … blah? You come and see me, okay? From now on it's my job to tell you when you're being dumb.'

She lets out a chuckle, and I join in too.

After school on Wednesday, I head to the library as if it's the most natural thing in the world. I'm much better prepared for the debate tomorrow, if I do say so myself.

The other two have their heads down, writing out phrases on cue cards. I spend time jotting words down too.

I'll start with the introduction, of course, which is boring enough to learn off by heart. Chairperson, members of the audience, etc. etc. All I write is 'Intro' because I know I'll remember the rest.

Then I move on to the ideas we came up with after I spoke to Mr Chiu. I've scrawled down three of the points when Zara looks up from her paper.

'Shall we start?' She turns to me. 'Want to go first, Phoebs?'

'No, you go …' But then I change my mind. I'll be doing this speech in front of a whole crowd of strangers tomorrow – I need all the practice I can get.

Zara tells me to choose any place that I'll be comfortable, so I find a spot at the end of the table and sit. Standing seems like overkill now.

I hold my cue cards and read 'Intro' as a prompt for my first line: 'Chairperson, members of the audience …' There's this nervous wobble in my voice. I glance up at Jagath and Zara, who both nod encouragingly.

Ignoring the wobble, I keep going.

The others stop me with a tip here or a suggestion there, but I feel pretty good about it. Then we go through some of the rebuttals I could use against the opposition.

Zara goes through her speech again. It's the same as we heard on the weekend, except this time she's added bits into the gaps and found better ways to say other parts. At one point I stop her with an idea. She nods eagerly, adding it straight onto her cue card.

Then the meeting finishes and my heart skips. I think I'm ready.

Like last week, Jagath and I walk out together. When we reach the front gate, he gestures towards a white station wagon at the curb. 'That's Mum.'

'Oh, okay.' I try not to sound disappointed. 'See you at the debate.' I prop my foot against the fence.

'You bet.'

I'm checking up the street for Dad when a door slams and I turn to see Jagath returning my way. 'Mum wants to know if you need a lift tomorrow.'

'Dad's going to drive me.' He was fine about it last

night when I checked. My eyes track a passing car as my mind ticks over. 'But that would save him taking more time off work …'

'It's no trouble.'

The more I think about this, the more I like the idea. A lift with Jagath means more time together. There's another car going past; this one's Dad's. Good timing.

Dad's car slows as I wave, and then pulls into a No Parking zone.

'I'll ask. Okay?'

Together we make our way over. Dad stays sitting in the driver's seat and winds his window down.

'Hey, Dad, this is Jagath.'

'Pleased to meet you.' Jagath moves one arm forward slightly, which Dad ignores.

'And this is, ah … Stavros.'

A pause. Dad doesn't even respond. I decide to push through. 'Jagath's mum has offered to drive me to the debate tomorrow. And I thought –'

'No. I'm taking you,' Dad says straight out. 'We discussed this already.' It's beginning to feel weird, because

Dad still hasn't looked at Jagath. Just slightly, Dad's expression flickers towards him. 'But thank you.'

Dad looks back to me, as if everything's normal. Like this is how my family speaks all the time.

'Yeah, I just thought it would save you taking time off –'

'*Sta echo pee. Tora bess sto aftokinito.*' Dad says over the top of me. 'We've discussed this already. Now get in the car.'

I actually blink before focusing on Dad again. How could he do that? Speak Greek in front of someone who can't understand? Like slamming a door in his face.

I can't even look at Jagath. I think about translating for him. But that would be weird and now my pause is making it worse, so I just mumble: 'Okay.'

I turn to Jagath, cheeks hot, but trying to act as if nothing just happened. 'Thanks anyway.'

'No problem.' Jagath nods. 'See you tomorrow.'

As soon as he turns, I walk around to the passenger seat of our car. My whole body burns with anger. I can't believe Dad just did that.

Chapter Eight

The whole way home, I say nothing. Unless you count the single grunt I make when Dad asks about the meeting. That's the way we answer in this family when we don't like the question, isn't it? I've learnt from the expert.

As soon as we pile through the front door, Dad fills a pot with water to boil and sets about chopping. Tomatoes, garlic and basil.

Lucky. If dinner were up to me, he'd be going hungry.

Dad serves up and we all sit in the living room with bowls on knees. The news starts but Steph barely stops chatting. All she gets out of me are *hmms* and *ah-huhs*.

The opening segment is about a demonstration in Sydney. Three people injured. There's a clip of the organiser shaking his head, saying how frustrated he is that their protest turned violent: 'An angry few wrecking it for everyone else.'

I eat my pasta without tasting it. Don't look at Dad.

We move through more segments and come to an update about the wild berries that lower blood pressure. Another doctor this time, saying that the current medicine is just as effective as the berries, and cheaper to produce.

This doctor is way chubby, if you ask me, fair skin and grey hair. 'Don't waste your time berry-hunting just yet …' he says with a smarmy smile.

Dad jerks his fork at the TV, chewing. 'What did I tell you?' he says out the side of his mouth. 'The other one had no idea.'

I look right at Dad. 'Yeah, the Indian doctor had no idea. Clearly.' But my voice is cool.

I watch Dad's reaction but he just keeps eating, eyes on the TV. As if the words I said were completely fine. Utterly normal.

'He probably got his medical degree out of a cereal packet,' I say, louder this time.

Dad stops eating and turns my way. 'What's up with you?'

'Nothing.' But it comes out cold.

Dad swallows, still watching me, frowning slightly.

'That's what we do, isn't it? Take one look at a person and make up our mind? Decide they're not worth listening to?'

Dad shakes his head. 'What are you talking about?'

The confusion in his eyes makes me nervous, because I'm not sure what to say next. I've never told Dad that I think he's wrong before. But I've come this far. My head lifts. 'I can't believe you did that today,' I say evenly.

Dad frowns. 'What did I do?'

'You spoke Greek in front of Jagath and totally shut him out.'

Dad's expression darkens. 'I was speaking to you.'

'So? I speak English too, or haven't you noticed?'

'You want me to yell at you in front of your friends?'

'It was so embarrassing!'

Creases deepen on Dad's forehead. 'You're embarrassed by your own father?'

Sometimes. Yes. 'You'd never do that to Mum. You always make sure she understands.'

'That's different.'

Steph is staring across at us with her mouth open, a single tube of pasta jammed on her fork.

'Put it this way,' I say slowly. 'How would you feel if Jagath's parents didn't like me because I'm half-Greek? If *they* avoided looking at *me*?'

Dad snorts. 'They can do what they like.'

I search for situations that he'll understand. 'Or they decide that since you're Greek, they'll just call you Con.' They're all there, and I feel them bubbling to the surface. I don't have to search far. 'Or they call you a greasy Greek or … or … Gorilla Girl, and they …'

And there, in the middle of the sentence, I stop. They laugh at your hairy arms …

I don't have to look far because they're right there, in my memory. I was teased for weeks in grade five. That was before I wore make-up to school, before I started reading

Glamour Girl. Before some bunch of kids came up with that name, I hadn't even noticed how hairy I was.

'Phoebe!' Dad shakes his head, angry and maybe a little lost. 'I've heard all that and then some! Been passed over when waiting to be served in shops ...'

I shake my head. 'How could you treat Jagath like that?'

Dad's eyes narrow, his jaw muscles clenching, and I wonder if maybe I've made my point. But then he says, 'That's different.' He picks up his bowl and stands, even though he hasn't finished.

'I have nothing against him, all right? I'm just saying they're different.' Dad strides into the kitchen.

I can feel Steph watching me, but I'm too annoyed to make eye contact. I stand up. I can't leave it there. Every idea, every perspective, has a right to be heard.

Dad glances up when I come into the kitchen.

'What do you mean it's different?' I say. 'How can you be so sure that you don't like him unless you get to know him first?'

'*Stamata,*' he says. 'That's enough.' Then, 'Speak like that to me again and you go to your room.'

I take a breath, try to stay calm. 'I'm not …' I say quietly. And then louder: 'I'm just explaining what I –'

'*Stamata!*' Dad blasts.

This is so unfair. I glare at him.

He points with his arm straight and finger sharp. '*Fyge.*' 'Go.'

I'm only two steps away when movement in the living room catches my eye, just a flash. Steph was probably listening and just scurried away.

Slowly, I swivel to face Dad again.

'No.' Because he can't have it both ways. He can't treat me like a child now, just because I've made up my own mind, but treat me like a responsible adult when he needs my help with Steph. He can't have it both ways.

'I beg your pardon?' Dad says slowly.

'I've done nothing wrong. All I did was say what I –'

'Go to your room!' Dad strides around the bench and stops right in front of me. 'NOW!' It's so loud that I'm sure the walls actually expand and contract.

'No,' I say again, fists clenching but eyes watering. What will he do? Dad might be loud when he's angry, but he's never rough. He can't force me to go to my room.

And even though I'm scared of what's happening, I also feel something else, deep within. A surging kind of adrenaline. I'm standing up for what I think. I'm only using words, but I'm making an impact. Saying what I believe.

'You can't make me,' I say quietly.

Dad is almost panting; I imagine his breath as bursts of scalding steam. 'Go to your room, right now.'

'Or what? You'll ruin my life? You'll embarrass me in front of my friends?'

Dad actually flinches when I spit the last word. He turns slowly, deliberately, and steps towards my lunch box on the ledge. He lifts a yellow paper from inside: the signed registration form for tomorrow's debate.

Pinching the top tightly with his fingers, as if preparing to rip, he holds it high. 'Go to your room or I withdraw permission for tomorrow.'

'You can't do that!' I'm loud in my disbelief. 'I'm part of a team!'

'Then GO.'

Our eyes meet and I realise I have no choice. Seconds

later, a sob bursts from me. The frustration is too much to hold inside. I hate that I burst into tears in front of Dad.

I spin away, then turn back one last time, shooting him a glare through my watering eyes. A stab of anger. *You have no right.*

This time, we're not on the same side.

I reach my room, fly onto the bed and scream into my pillow.

It fades back to sobs but it all flows out. A stream of frustration. It feels good to let it out.

I roll on my side, calmer now, but still simmering. He has no right …

Someone taps at my door. So quietly that at first I wonder if it was just a creak of the house. Again, it comes: two tiny taps.

'Not now, Steph,' I say without moving. *Just leave me alone.*

I hold my breath, listening. Nothing more comes.

I don't even feel bad for sending her away. I'm tired of worrying about her. Ever since Mum's been sick, I've been there for Steph.

Ever since Mum's been sick, I've done my best.

Ever since she's been sick …

For some reason, tears flow again. Suddenly I'm annoyed at Mum, too, for a whole jumble of reasons. For letting Dad say the stuff he says, and letting us grow up thinking it was normal. And more than that. For always being there for us, letting me grow up thinking life was easy – and then just going away.

Right now, I don't even care that she had a good excuse; I know she didn't ask to get sick. But I didn't have a say in it either.

I lie on my side for a long time, doing nothing except staring and feeling like crap. I just want to go back to how it all used to be. When everything seemed simple and safe. When I could just be a kid.

When my legs begin to go stiff I sit up, hugging my pillow to my chest. There's no way I'm talking to Dad, ever again. Not until he listens to me.

〃

There's no way he's driving me to the debate tomorrow.

I grab my phone and select Jagath's name, feeling a fresh surge of adrenaline, as if simply calling him is a way to defy Dad.

'Hey, all set for tomorrow?' Jagath answers, straight out.

'Yep.' I bite my bottom lip, harder and harder, as tears once more start to flow. What the hell is wrong with me? I can hardly speak on the phone, let alone in front of a crowd.

'Are you okay?' Jagath sounds concerned.

Slowly I inhale. 'Can I catch a lift tomorrow?'

'Sure. We're meeting Zara at the school gate at eight-thirty. Can you get there on your own?'

'Yeah. Thanks.'

A pause. 'Is everything okay?'

'Yeah … it's just …' What can I say? 'I had a fight with Dad, that's all.'

'Not the best evening of the century, hey?' Jagath says quietly.

I'm glad he doesn't ask why. But talking helps. 'Yeah, he's a stubborn pig,' I say and half-laugh.

Jagath lets out a low chuckle. 'Sounds like my dad.'

'Your dad's a stubborn pig too?' I'm smiling.

'More an ancient dinosaur,' says Jagath. 'He thinks I should follow in his footsteps. Work with him in the hotel kitchen ... But with homework, guitar and debating, I just don't have time.'

'And you have other ideas?'

'You could say that.' Jagath pauses but I stay silent, hoping he'll keep going. 'I want to be a human-rights lawyer,' he says quietly. The tone in his voice makes me think he's sharing something close to his heart. A secret dream ...

'Wow,' I say. 'That's ...' Impressive. And big. The sort of dream someone who's going to make a difference in the world would have. 'You'll totally make it, Jagath.'

'I dunno,' Jagath mumbles. 'You need crazy marks to get into those courses at uni ...'

'You'll get there, I bet.'

'... but I'm going to try.'

'That's cool,' I say. I don't want to sound flippant, so I add, 'Really. I mean it.'

Jagath is quiet for a moment. 'So what do you want to be when – you know – when you grow up and all that?'

'Ah … don't know.' Until recently, I would have said hairdresser straight out. But now I'm not sure. Compared to a human-rights lawyer, hairdressing sounds completely lame. 'Something I'm good at, I guess …'

And even though I'm being vague, I think about Erin and Mr Mendes, the way they both encouraged me, and a tiny voice pipes up inside. *Maybe*, it whispers, *maybe you could …*

'Well, you're great at debating,' Jagath says. 'Ready for tomorrow?'

'Ready as I'll ever be,' I say. Though honestly I'm not sure I'm ready for anything.

'Good. Well. I'd better go,' Jagath says. 'See you at eight-thirty?'

'Yeah,' I say, my heart beating harder as I think about my talk tomorrow. I won't just be speaking in front of our class this time, but in front of kids from other schools. And adjudicators. People with lots of brains.

After I hang up, I pull out the cue cards for tomorrow

and stand in front of the mirror, skimming through my speech and pretending I'm in front of a crowd. I even practise gesturing with my hands to emphasise the big points. Sort of daggy, but it's not as if anyone can see me in here.

I'm in the middle of my conclusion when someone taps twice on my door. The door opens the tiniest gap, enough only for half of Steph's face to slide through in slow motion.

Her single eye lands on me and she lifts one arm, offering half a licorice stick. 'Want this?'

Dad gave Steph a licorice stick while I was stuck in my room? He has a stash hidden at the top of the pantry and nothing gets us bouncing around him faster than the crinkle of that bag.

I think about him sitting out there, watching TV, and the anger burns. It's not just what he did to Jagath, but the way he refused to listen to my point of view.

Steph's still waiting, so I sit on the bed and pat a space beside me. She bounds forward and proudly holds out the thick black stick. You can even see teeth marks at the place where she forced herself to stop.

'Why don't we go halves …' I break it in two, but Steph shakes her head when I hold out the quarter.

'No, I saved half for you.'

'Really?'

Steph adores licorice; normally she'd be gutsing her piece down and then scouting around for more. I can't help wondering how much she understood about my fight with Dad.

'Well, thanks,' I say.

Steph ends up accepting a small section at the end and we chew together, grinning at each other with black teeth. I don't feel quite as bad as I did before, but I can't stop thinking about the debate tomorrow.

After my argument with Dad, it seems more important than ever.

Chapter Nine

Steph's beside me when I wake the next morning, with just the tangled top of her hair showing. I slide out from under the covers, rocking the bed as little as possible, and sneak out to the bathroom.

I wash my hair and shave my legs and forearms. Halfway through, I pause, warm water falling around my shoulders. Stupid kids in grade five. They were the ones who first called me Gorilla Girl. They were just being idiots and probably don't even remember teasing me about my hairy arms. But now that I think about what happened, I realise that I've been giving them power over me, and letting *their* opinion of me mean more than my opinion of myself.

I want to take that power back, but I'm not sure how.

When I get to the kitchen Dad's unpacking the dishwasher. I make a beeline for my lunch box, pull out the permission form, fold it in four and slip it into the pocket of my blazer. Signed and ready. He can't tear it now.

'*Kalimera*,' he says, straightening up, with a pile of plates balanced on one arm. He's testing the water, I think. Checking to see how I'll respond.

'Morning,' I say into the fridge, grabbing an Up&Go.

'I'm taking the morning off work –' he begins to say, but I've already bolted for the living room.

'Phoebe!' Dad calls, but I just keep going as if I haven't heard. It's not like he ever stops and listens to me.

I organise my gear, brush my teeth and then head back to the kitchen.

'Phoebe,' Dad says with a tone of relief. 'What time does it –'

'Don't worry,' I say before he's even finished. 'I'm catching a lift with Jagath's mum, I've organised it already.'

I'm expecting him to try to stop me, but all he does is lift one hand. 'But I want to drive you …'

'No,' I say. 'I'd rather be with my friends.' The pain in his eyes sends a stab of guilt through me.

But I turn away. Head out the door. I'm not talking to him until he's ready to listen.

We make a pact not to talk about our debate during the trip to Archibald Hall. According to Zara, the last time the team did that they tied themselves up with nerves, lost their train of thought during the debate and totally messed up. Much better to trust our preparation, we decide, and focus on staying calm.

Jagath's in the front seat with me diagonally behind him in the back. My hands are clasped tightly in my lap. A ball of energy sits in my chest, waiting like a racehorse in the starting gates. As long as I don't let it bolt, I think I'll be okay.

Zara does most of the talking during the trip, about

a public-speaking competition later in the year. Jagath's mum asks about junior band and Zara chats happily about some trumpet player with freakish talent.

Jagath keeps turning his head, listening to Zara, but every now and then he makes eye contact and I'm hit with the sense that he's checking to see if I'm okay. Or maybe he's just making sure I'm not so nervous that I throw up in his mum's car.

Jagath's mum pulls up right at the entrance and we all pile out. She drives off to park and I follow the others through the foyer and into the auditorium. There are masses of seats all sloping down towards a stage.

This place is huge.

Even worse, debaters are everywhere. All in uniform, of course. I've always thought ours was lame, but I have to admit that some of the other schools' uniforms are okay. So serious. And intimidating.

The uniforms give everyone this total air of confidence, as if they're the sort of people who know who they are and where they're going. The sort of students who enter interschool debates and win.

A hand presses on my back. 'It seems much worse from here,' Zara says.

Jagath steps forward, blocking out the hall and enclosing us in a circle. Just the three of us.

'Yeah, it'll be easier once we're on stage. You can hardly see the audience then,' he says.

'Hope so ...' I snort and let out a laugh.

Jagath smiles. 'How about a drink?'

With her hand still resting on my back, Zara guides me to a cafe at one end of the foyer. Jagath sticks close on my other side. Three of us walking in a row. The McEwan College Junior Debating Team.

'I'll get drinks. Coffee? Orange juice?' Zara asks once we find a table. 'Nothing with bubbles,' she adds. 'Unless you want to burp at the wrong moment.'

'Ahhh ...' I don't really feel like anything. I scan the board, pulling coins out of my side pocket. 'Maybe just an OJ?'

I hand her some coins and Zara heads over to the counter while Jagath and I sit next to each other at a table. As we settle in, our eyes meet.

Jagath leans towards me. 'How're you doing?'

He's not just talking about the debate. I rest my elbows on the table. Our arms are close. 'Don't know, really.' I can't think about Dad right now, not with the debate looming. It's as if he's the last brick in my tower. If I let myself focus on last night, my world will come crumbling down.

'It'll be okay,' Jagath says, and I feel the faintest brush of his arm. 'Trust me.'

'Yeah.' I even manage a smile, because I do trust him. I'm not looking at him when I say it, though. I'm staring at our hands resting back to back on the table, so close that our skin tones stand out in contrast. Mine pale like coffee cream, and his dark like chocolate.

Before I know what's happening, his arm shifts ever so slightly closer to mine and his fingertips brush against the back of my hand.

It's a shy sort of question. *Are you …?*

Could we …?

My skin tingles. But then I go cold. Goosepimply. A realisation hits me. *He likes me. He likes me. He likes me.*

Suddenly, it's all too much to take in. Fighting with

Dad last night, being here now, Mum still not home. It's as if my brain has hit overload. Jagath's so amazing, but I can't deal with this right now.

I'm not even sure what to think, let alone what to feel. My cheeks flush as I pull my hand back, clearing my throat as if nothing happened.

Our eyes meet again but this time, it is awkward. Jagath goes to speak but then his mouth sort of droops. He just asked a question without words, so what can he say now?

His arm pulls back like mine did, and we're left sitting together as we were before, except now there's a huge chasm between us.

'Those drinks sure are taking a while,' Jagath says softly, craning to see across the room.

'Yeah. What time do we start again?' I ask, even though I know exactly.

'Eleven. But we'll have to wait through the first round,' Jagath says.

I summon the courage to glance at him and smile, trying to show that I've just been caught unawares, but he quickly turns away. It's clear from the way he's avoiding my eyes that he knows I understood his question and he thinks I've turned him down. Jagath's not dumb.

Neither am I. If I hadn't freaked out and pulled my hand away, everything could be different right now.

All through the first round we act as if nothing happened, but the whole time I'm aware of Jagath sitting in the audience beside me. My private radar of the world does a *blip* each time it circles past him.

We sit in a row, with me in the middle, and Zara leaning in to whisper pointers: why going over time is a bad idea, even though you don't lose marks, how one guy who keeps cracking jokes is letting his side down, and how another girl who pauses during two key moments is one of the best debaters she's ever seen. Jagath keeps quiet.

The first round finishes and the audience transforms into a mass of moving bodies. Our team heads around to the waiting area. Zara ducks into the toilets and I realise Jagath and I are about to be left alone.

'Wait up!' I call to Zara and dash in after her. I can't talk to Jagath now.

When I'm locked in a stall I take time to focus, breathing slowly in and out as I imagine myself on stage, convincing the audience of our argument.

I'm here to do a job: second affirmative speaker. I want to do it well.

The first debate starts up and we wait in a side room. We're next in line. Zara charts a circuit of the room, muttering through her opening and gesturing at the walls. Mr Mendes pokes his head in to say good luck and then disappears. Jagath sits frozen still, frowning into space as he listens to the action on stage. He can't prepare much now; it's his job to refute the other team's points, so he can't plan anything until he hears them speak.

Applause bursts out at the end of the first debate, and my heart beats harder, anticipating the moment when I'm standing behind the lectern.

We troop on stage in a line, Zara first, then me, and Jagath last, while the opposition team marches on from the other side: two guys and a girl. As they take their seats, the guy at the front eyeballs Zara, trying to psych her out. The girl at the end is so tense that she's almost robotic.

The debate is introduced by a woman in a navy dress suit. Then Zara stands, moving away from the safety of our team and making her way to the lectern. With her, I turn to the audience.

Oh my gosh. First speaker has it tough.

'Chairperson, members of the audience,' Zara begins. 'Our topic for debate today is that uniforms should be compulsory in all schools.' She pauses and casts her gaze over the audience. 'Let me be clear. We're not saying that uniforms serve a purpose in just *some* cases. We will demonstrate today why uniforms are effective when worn by all students. Because that's what a uniform does: it unites us.'

She's calm and clear, with just the right touch of earnestness. Zara continues through a summary of her points, then moves on to introduce the rest of the team before starting into her main argument.

As Zara speaks, I scan the audience, trying to gauge their reaction. It's clear she's making an impact. Every now and then the adjudicators write a note. Students from the other team keep whispering. Most people in the audience sit motionless, taking in Zara's every word.

'Sure, we love to express our individual tastes on the weekend. Doesn't everyone?' Zara continues as a ripple of agreement goes through the room. 'There is a place for bikinis and baseball caps. But that place is not school ...'

I've almost scanned the whole auditorium when I spot a familiar face. I blink, peering through the downlights ...

Dad?

He's on his own, second row from the front, wearing a black business suit. At the sight of him sitting there, my pulse explodes. I told him not to come.

The crowd applauds at the end of Zara's speech and she returns to our table. I pull my eyes away from Dad to congratulate her but I can't stop my eyes looking back to him.

Even though we're in a hall full of people, all I can see is Dad. It's as if he's in the spotlight, lit up against the sea of uniforms. Not a student. Not a teacher. He doesn't even seem to belong with the other parents in casual clothes.

And even though I'm still angry with him, I'm hit with a wave of guilt for telling him I was embarrassed by him, that I didn't want him to come.

It's only when there's applause for a second time that I realise it's my turn. All eyes turn my way when I stand. As if in a dream, I float to the lectern. None of this is real. I've been so busy thinking about Dad that I'm not even nervous. It's like I'm only half-here.

It seems like minutes before I actually come to a stop behind the lectern. I rest my cue cards against the top and then, finally, stare out at the sea of faces. Now is my time.

Except, I have nothing. I'm completely blank.

Breathing fast, I check the cue cards: Intro. Unite. I can barely work out what I was thinking. It's a jumble of scribbled words that mean nothing to me now.

I look up again at the faces watching me expectantly. Panic engulfs my mind. Pounding heart and sweaty palms. All I can hear is my heartbeat.

The clunk of a chair being moved on stage makes me turn and I see Zara nod encouragingly.

My focus moves to Jagath. This time, he doesn't look

away. His head dips, urging me on, and now more than ever I'm hit with the sense of what it means to be a member of this team, part of something I care about.

More than anything, I don't want to let them down.

I turn back to the audience and breathe in. So many faces waiting for me. Among them all is my dad. I told him not to come, but he did. To hear me speak.

That's when I find my voice.

Chapter Ten

'Picture a world where we all look the same.'

There's an intake of breath from Zara behind me as soon as I speak, but she doesn't need to worry. I know I've broken the template, but I feel sure about what I'm going to say, and this is the best way to start.

'A world where we look exactly alike,' I say again. 'How would we tell who was who?' I scan the audience, giving them time to consider. 'We'd have to talk to each other, for a start. We'd have to find a way to see beyond our appearances. We'd begin to relate to each other in terms of who we are on the inside. Can you imagine?'

I take a breath. 'This, Chairperson, members of the audience ... this is why we need uniforms in schools. They help us see beyond our physical differences. They encourage us to find connections and relate to each other in terms of our opinions, our ideas, our hopes and dreams.'

Again, I pause. 'Our first speaker has already demonstrated that uniforms are an important aspect of school life ...'

When I get to that part, there's a faint sigh of relief from Zara behind me, because I'm back in the template. She never needed to worry. I may have bent the rules in the way I began, but that was just my way of getting everyone's attention. I'm still working within the rules, just in my own unique way.

Now that I've found my opening, the whole speech falls into place. I've read through it so often, and thought about it from so many angles, that I don't need cue cards to prompt me. I know this topic back to front.

As I continue I'm conscious of the whole room. I'm holding their attention, pulling it tight like string, or relaxing it to let them digest.

I'm aware of the whole space, of people sitting way up in the back row, and sitting on either side. Even the adjudicators, who seemed so spooky-intimidating, are on the end of my string. I have a sense of the entire auditorium, but most of all I'm aware of Dad. The place where he's sitting is lit up in my mind. I've got his attention most of all, because I'm not only talking about uniforms and the clothes we wear. I'm also talking about skin colour. Background too.

Imagine a world where you can't see nationality at a glance, I try to tell him, where you see nothing about a person's background just from looking at them. There's so much more to each of us than the way we look …

He might not understand the double meaning to my speech, and even if he did, I know he wouldn't agree. But at least this time I have the chance to tell him what I think.

This time, he can't send me to my room.

I'm also meant to point out reasons why the opposition's argument is wrong, and even though I was focused on Dad while their first speaker was on, I did pick up familiar phrases from his speech.

This is a free country.

We should be allowed to express ourselves.

We are all unique.

I'm pretty clear about some things he said, actually, because I know his side of the argument inside out. I mostly agree with that point of view and, somehow, that makes it easier to argue against. In another place, during another debate, the person arguing their case could be me.

So I don't even try to argue that the opposition is wrong, I just point out there's a time and place for expressing ourselves by the clothes we wear, and that's outside school. At school, uniforms put us on equal ground and allow us to express our uniqueness through our thoughts and actions, not just our clothes.

I've nearly finished speaking when a chime rings out, signalling that my time is almost up. It feels like I've climbed a mountain in that time but I don't panic, just move naturally to my conclusion.

'We stand before you,' I say and gesture to include Zara and Jagath, 'united in our conviction that uniforms should be compulsory in schools. We are also united by the very clothes we wear. We are the team for the affirmative, and our uniform unites us.'

I nod in thanks and then take my seat as applause erupts. I'm buzzing and light and almost disappointed to be sitting back down.

That was way better than doing a speech in class. I had the whole auditorium listening to me. They may not have agreed with every point, but maybe, just maybe, I persuaded one or two to see it differently.

Zara squeezes me around the shoulders. 'Talk about a rollercoaster ride,' she whispers with a gush in my ear.

The applause dies down as the second speaker for the opposition stands to speak. I turn to Jagath. He nods slightly, but his eyes linger on mine and I want so much to talk to him properly. I can't now, though, not here.

I take a breath and face the front again. The opposition is speaking again and we all focus. I keep busy jotting down ideas for Jagath's rebuttal, passing Zara's ideas to him with my own. Our first two speeches might be over, but our team is far from finished.

Every now and then I glance up at Dad in the audience.

He's already heard me speak so I'm half-expecting him to disappear back to work, but each time I look I find him standing out among the others, listening to the end.

Dad's in the middle of the foyer when we come out.

I slow my pace and turn to Zara and Jagath. 'Better go. Say thanks to your mum for the ride in.' I tell Jagath.

'And we'll see you at school!' Zara flings her arms around my neck and rocks from side to side. 'Don't forget, next Wednesday …'

'… team meeting,' I finish, after coming up for air. No time to celebrate our victory. We're through to regionals, which apparently includes something called a 'secret-topic debate'. Terrifying. And sort of intriguing …

Zara pulls away and I turn to Jagath, lifting my arms as if a hug goodbye is the most natural thing to do. We're fellow debate winners, wartime survivors.

But Jagath stiffens slightly, and that moment in the cafe comes back in a rush.

I drop both arms and tilt my head. 'See you at school?'

Which also means, *Are we okay?* I want to ask more than that, so much more, but I can't in front of Zara. Definitely not in front of Dad.

'Sure.' Jagath nods. But I can't read his face.

I make my way over to Dad and stop in front of him, feeling suddenly awkward with him here among the crowd.

'You came,' is all I manage.

His jaw muscles clench. 'Of course.'

We turn together and make our way through the exit. We're already starting down the steps when Dad clears his throat. 'Congratulations, *koukla*. Your win was … impressive.'

'Thanks.' I pause and glance back towards the foyer where I left Jagath. When I swivel back, Dad's waiting a couple of steps down.

'It was a team effort,' I say and start towards him.

'I know …'

Then we go quiet, as if there's this weight hanging in the air between us. We turn away from the car park for

Archibald Hall and head towards a side street, walking side by side.

After a while, Dad says, 'Your friend, this Jag-at.' The name comes out awkwardly. 'You think I insulted him?'

'I don't know …' I haven't asked Jagath about that yet. But that's not the only reason I was upset. It was also because Dad didn't give me a chance to explain what I was trying to say.

We near the car and Dad bips it open. Instead of starting the engine once we're in, Dad turns to me, keys still in his hand.

'I'm sorry I embarrassed you.' He says it slowly. 'I know I don't always act the right way, I'm not … relaxed around strangers.'

He waits for my response, so I nod. It's not easy getting to know new people. Don't I know that.

'Growing up in Greece,' Dad continues, 'we had family all around, people I knew. But here … it's not the same.'

'Yeah, I know.' I check out my hands in my lap, feeling weird to have made Dad explain himself like this but, at the same time, wanting him to keep going.

Dad slips the key into the ignition. 'To me, family is all that matters. More than anything.' He shrugs as if it's settled now, and turns the key.

The engine hums to life while I just sit there. That's it? He still hasn't tried to understand my side. Not really. He might have explained why he says the things he does, but that still doesn't make it right.

Frustration bubbles in me, but I'm not angry like I was last night. More … I don't know, like I'm seeing the world through slightly more grown-up eyes. It's as if I'm standing in the middle of a seesaw, starting on my side and then leaning the other way, trying to see it from Dad's point of view.

Coming to Australia when he was still learning the language. People hearing his accent and assuming they wouldn't understand. Being called names …

Maybe that's why he finds it hard to trust strangers, people who seem different from him.

And even though I wonder if he'll ever understand what it's like on my side of the seesaw, I want him to know that I'm sorry I told him not to come to the debate. I want to tell him that although these past months have been the worst in my life, worrying that Mum might never come home, in some ways they've been the best, because through all this Dad and I have been a team. We've been through our own family's war zone, and we're almost out the other side. Stronger, now. All of us, not just Mum.

For a moment the dream feels so close that I can reach out and brush a fingertip against it. The day that Mum would be home, for good.

'But, what about … Mum?' I say, picking up the conversation where we left off. 'She's family …' I pause. 'But she hasn't always been. And you trust her.' She didn't grow up in Greece, so she counts as different. At least, different from Dad.

For a while, Dad's quiet. I watch his face side on, seeing the wrinkles and lines deepen into a smile. 'Your mother's one of a kind.'

'Yes, but how did you work that out?' I'm onto him straight away, even though I know the answer.

I never get sick of hearing how they met: Dad lost and struggling to ask for directions, and Mum walking him all the way to the right building at uni. In the time it took them to go from one side of campus to the other, they'd started a conversation that's still going today. I'll never get tired of hearing their voices go quiet and gentle when they talk to each other.

'I worked out your mum was special,' Dad says slowly, 'when I got to know her.'

And all I hear is the humming of the engine.

I'm not sure if Dad realises what he just said but his eyes flicker towards me, then back to the road. I can see him thinking it through. He's just echoed the words I asked him last night: *How can you be so sure that you don't like someone unless you get to know them?*

'Listen, Phoebe,' Dad says after a while. 'You know I'm proud of you, don't you? Not just today, but proud every day.' He makes a point of looking right at me, making sure I understand.

I smile back, nodding awkwardly, not sure how to respond. He's never said that before. But it's easier between us now. I managed to explain to him how I feel and this time, he listened. For now, that's enough.

Chapter Eleven

Early the next morning, my eyes flutter open. There's a small smile on my lips, thinking about Jagath.

Now that the debate is over, I'm able to think properly about what happened. He did pick up on the vibe between us. He must have. Somehow I have to show him that I pulled away out of surprise, not because I don't like him back.

I shower quickly, humming as I shave my legs and arms. I rub down with a towel, moisturise, then blow-dry my hair. Once finished, I wipe mist from the mirror and stare at my reflection.

Right now, I feel really good about the person who stares back. She feels strong from the inside out. This is the way to get back my power, I decide. By looking good and feeling good, but doing it for myself, not because I'm worried what anyone else thinks.

Instead of packing my magic bag of make-up tricks, I spend time fixing my hair with pins – neat but with a touch of style. It's part of me that I've always been glad to have. The part that shows I'm half-Greek.

The part I get from Dad.

He's stacking the dishwasher when I make it to the kitchen.

'Sleep okay, *koukla*?' asks Dad, drying his hands on a tea towel.

'Slept great.' We're out of Up&Go so I grab the last two slices of bread from the freezer and drop them in the toaster. Fresh bread hasn't been a top priority on The List.

'I've put on a load of washing,' Dad says. 'But that's the last of the bread, so …' He pulls some money from his pocket. 'Want to buy lunch?'

'Really?' Steph's head pops up over the back of the couch.

'We're having a LUNCH ORDER!'

She gets busy writing hers out while I slip a note and some coins in my pocket. 'I'll do the pick-up?' I ask Dad.

One nod. 'And I'll take Steph to school,' he says.

We smile at each other then, aware that this is the last day we'll be working through The List on our own. When Mum comes home tomorrow, everything will change. But she'll still need rest, so we won't go back to the way things used to be. And I don't think I'd want that, even if we could.

I keep an eye out for Jagath as we traipse into the hall for Friday morning assembly. Briana's busy chatting about volleyball. I guide our group towards seats at the back of our year level, so we have a view of everything without being expected to join in.

Mr Chiu takes us through the usual boring stuff, excursions for next week, something about hockey training. He welcomes back the year nines and tens from science camp and Erin gets the wriggles.

Then Mr Mendes takes the microphone and I take the chance to vague out, scanning the rows in front of me for Jagath's black hair. But I can't find him in the crowd.

It's only when I hear the phrase 'junior debating team' that my ears zing to the front.

'The adjudicators' report came back,' announces Mr Mendes, 'and I'm proud to announce that our team achieved the highest score of the day. Please come down and accept your certificates, Zara Waters, Jagath Rajapakse and Phoebe Cholas.'

Around me, people clap half-heartedly. A prickle of warmth rises up my neck to my face. Pretty sure I'm now a lovely shade of beetroot.

'Go on, Phoebe!' Briana has grabbed my wrist, stepped out from her seat and is pulling me up.

Sheepishly, I start down the steps. Everyone is watching. I'm halfway down when I register the blond hair of the guy whose locker is next to mine. Even from the side I can tell it's him. He's sitting with two mates, their heads leaning over a phone.

Something makes him look up as I pass, but this time I'm the first one to glance away. I jog down the rest of the stairs like a slingshot that's been released. Why should I care what he thinks? I hardly even know the guy.

Jagath and Zara are already on stage and their expressions lift me up. Mr Mendes shakes my hand before holding out the certificate. Mr Chiu makes a point of shaking our hands too, and then we all stand in a group, posing for photos for the school newsletter.

'I have a good feeling about this,' Zara whispers at one point. 'Regionals, here we come.'

It's awesome, I have to admit. Better than awesome – I'm part of something. I'm so busy grinning for photos that I don't have time to worry what other people are thinking. I'm too busy sharing the moment with people who matter.

Mr Chiu finishes the assembly, and everyone begins trudging out to first period. Zara winks my way before heading over to speak to a couple of year ten girls who I recognise from the debate.

Jagath has already turned away when I call out, 'Wait, Jagath?' He turns back and I have the sudden need to fidget. I jam both my hands behind my back. Be cool and casual. 'I just want to say thanks for all your help. You really saved me … I mean … you were great.'

His head tilts to one side. 'You were pretty good yourself.'

'So, I was wondering,' I push a hand into my pocket, checking that my money's still there. 'Do you want to meet in the canteen for lunch? Special today is chicken souvlaki …'

Jagath's head swaps to the other side, and the smile fades. 'Well, I'm a vegetarian so …'

And I just invited him to eat chicken? *Gulp*.

'Hey, don't stress. They do a pretty good vegie lasagne, too,' Jagath smiles. 'We could still meet …'

My heart leaps. 'Really?'

'You bet.' Jagath nods.

Those black eyes lock onto me, and I find myself smiling on the outside and melting within. I can't help it. Right now, I'm the happiest girl in the universe.

'See you at lunch.'

I spin away to find Briana and Erin waiting to one side. Still grinning, I bound over. Something tells me it's going to take a street sweeper to wipe this smile off my face.

'What was that all about?' they both say at the same time. I can tell from Briana's wide-open eyes that they've been watching for a while.

I put one arm around Briana and then the other around Erin, 'You'll never guess …'

At the end of the day, I'm still grinning. Lunch with Jagath was fun. We spoke about the debate for a bit, and then I listed all the Greek vegie dishes he has to try. I even summoned up the courage to ask why he's a vegetarian, and he told me about being Buddhist.

It wasn't a big deal, really. Nothing happened exactly. But somehow, it felt as if we were just a little closer to each other at the end of lunch than we were at the start. Each time I shared an opinion or learnt something new about Jagath, it was as if we took one small step closer to each other. Sentence by sentence. Idea by idea. Dream by dream.

Steph's all bouncy about Mum coming home when I pick her up, so I manage to talk her into helping me tidy up before tomorrow.

Easier said than done. She's still bargaining with me when I unlock the front door, asking how many minutes she can stay up tonight as payment for her work.

'What if I help clean the bathroom too?' Steph asks behind me. 'That counts for half an hour later to bed.'

'Twenty minutes, max,' I say, opening the door.

It hits me as soon I step inside – the smells of Sunday morning, that warm sense of home …

'MUM!' Steph screams and flashes past me, flying straight into Mum's outstretched arms. She's here! She's actually here.

Steph holds on for so long that I have to fight the urge to prise her off. *Not too tight, she'll break*, I want to say. Finally Steph comes up for air and I reach in for my hug.

Mum's shoulders feel bony and brittle, but she smells like melted butter.

'I couldn't stand it another day,' Mum smiles wearily once I pull back.

'You're here, you're here!' Steph bounces around us like a pogo stick. 'Can I call Dad?'

I know why. The idea of finally being together, at home again, might not seem like much. But right now I can't imagine anything better.

'He'll be home later.' Mum's voice is calm, understanding. She rubs her hands together as her eyes follow Steph: up, down, up. 'How about you stop bouncing, and help me make pikelets?'

The batter's waiting on the bench, so it's not long until warm cooking smells fill the air. We sit around the bench, happily licking butter off our fingers.

The fruit bowl is full, I notice as I gobble pikelets. Apples, bananas, even grapes. A fresh loaf of bread sits on the bench. Even the pile of empty cereal boxes and old newspapers has disappeared.

I turn to Mum guiltily. 'Have you been cleaning?'

'Celia drove me here,' she says. 'She straightened out a few things and she'll be dropping round every few days, but …' Mum leans back. 'Something tells me I have all the help I need right here.'

We've polished off the mountain of pikelets when Steph asks to watch TV. She ends up drifting from that room to this, enjoying the return to normal life, I guess, and savouring the sight of Mum here. Home, at last.

We tidy up and then Mum settles onto a bench chair, opposite me.

'So,' she says, fixing me with a smile. 'Tell me, how was your day?'

It's the simplest of questions, but I'm in the middle of so many things that I'm not sure where to start. And there's so much I want to tell her, now that we're alone.

About realising I'm actually good at something that I care about. The way it feels when I'm speaking in front of an audience. About Erin, who's not from a different planet after all. Maybe I'm more like her than I realised. And Jagath. Especially Jagath.

I also want to ask her what she thinks about the stuff that Dad says.

I've only paused a few moments when tears glisten and spill out from Mum's eyes, as if she knows exactly why I paused, just how much she's missed. All the times we've come home from school and she hasn't been here. All the conversations about little daily events that we haven't shared.

I get off the stool and wrap an arm protectively around her shoulders.

'No, no.' Mum shakes her head. 'I'm all right. Really. I've spent long enough being looked after …' She pulls away from me, and gets up to switch on the kettle, wiping her wet cheeks with the backs of her hands.

Soon she comes back to the bench, and places a warm mug of hot chocolate in front of me. Once again, she settles onto her stool.

'Take two.' Mum looks at me. 'So. How was your day, Phoebe?'

The hot chocolate is sweet and warm, made the way only Mum knows how. I lick froth from my lip.

Then I begin to speak.

The End

WANT MORE GIRL VS THE WORLD?

Hazel's friends are super-cool, but she feels like a fraud – she has no idea why they hang out with her. While they're all really grown-up, she doesn't even have her period yet. And she's not confident or pretty like they are, either.

Her friends make talking to boys look so easy, and even Hazel's mum has a new boyfriend, but Hazel doesn't think she's ever going to get kissed.

She's seriously crushing on Leo, who's sweet and funny and impossibly cute, but he's also in the year above. Why on earth would he be interested in Hazel?

For a sneak preview of this book, turn the page!

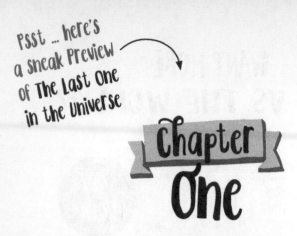

Psst ... here's a sneak preview of The Last One in the Universe

Chapter
One

Alice Carter was the most popular girl at our primary school, so it's weird knowing she hasn't even squeezed into the top twenty now that we're at high school. She's number twenty-three.

We know this because the boys made a 'hot list' for our year level. It was stuck up next to the timetables on the school events noticeboard. Even though it was taken down quickly – I think it only lasted three hours – pretty much everyone can remember the order.

I pretended not to notice that I was number seventeen.

1

There were forty girls on the list, so I was in the top half, but still … I felt a long way down.

At least I was put above Alice on the list. I mean, that surprised me at first. But I've learnt the rules are different in high school.

I know lists like that are stupid, of course. And cruel, particularly if you happen to rank very low. But the thing is, stupid or cruel or whatever, I don't reckon there was a single girl in our year who could help looking at that list. The worst thing would be not to have made it onto the list at all. That would be like you didn't even exist!

I can see Alice now as I walk across the quadrangle. She's hugging her books to her chest and looks like she's confused about *everything,* and that doesn't just mean what class she's got next, or where on earth it actually is.

'Hazel!' Alice turns and looks at me as though I'm a lifesaver. 'Do you mind walking with me to maths? I don't know where D12 is.'

Her eyes are darting around as though she thinks I might say no. Which I wouldn't, of course, but it makes her seem unconfident. Plus, her school dress is so long it meets up with her socks with no gap in between.

'Sure,' I say. D12 is one of those portable classrooms the school brought in a couple of weeks ago and plonked at the side of the oval. 'I just have to grab some books from my locker. Wanna come?'

'That would be awesome. Thanks, Hazel!'

I wish for her sake that she'd calm down a bit, but it doesn't seem likely. Alice is kind of bouncy, and always has been. It's one of the things that everyone loved about her in primary school. She pretty much had no vacancies for friends then. People hung around her all the time, and I never really got a chance to get close to her.

But these days, Alice drifts from group to group, like she doesn't quite belong anywhere.

Somehow I've landed on my feet. Not firmly, solidly, on my feet. More like a wobbly, *Oh my god, how is it that I'm in the popular group?* sort of landing. A *will I be able to keep this up?* sort of landing.

But it's way better than not landing at all. There were a couple of spooky months there while I went from group to group at lunchtime, trying to find somewhere to fit.

'It's so hard remembering where everything is, don't you think?' Alice says, interrupting my thoughts as we walk down the breezeway towards the lockers.

She doesn't wait for a response. 'It's like, you just get used to maths being in B block and then they change it and you're supposed to find somewhere else completely. And I really struggled with the homework Mr Cartwright set. Did you get the answer to that last question?'

'Scusi.' Ella Ingram pushes past me to get to her locker. She gets her books and turns around. Ella was number four on the hot list. I guess I can see why, but her face is pretty ordinary. Nothing really stands out there. Her hair isn't that different to mine. It's sort of mid-length and browny blonde and she wears it in a ponytail with blue clips at the sides. But I don't think the reason she made number four has anything to do with her face or her hair. Her school jumper is tucked up twice, like mine is. But it's way tighter, like mine would be if Mum had let me get the size I wanted. And her skirt only comes halfway down her thighs. You can see that Ella's got proper boobs, a proper waist and really long legs.

I haven't bothered asking Mum to take up my skirt. She'd probably say no, and even if she said yes, she'd never get around to it. She's too busy now that she's got a stupid boyfriend.

'So?' Alice prompts me. 'The last question?'

I watch as Ella heads off with her books.

'We have until the end of the week, Alice,' I say, turning to her. 'I haven't started it yet.'

Alice looks surprised. To be honest, I *have* done the homework sheet, except for the tricky last question, but there are people all around us and I don't want them to think I'm super keen or anything.

I get my books. Alice stands beside me, quietly now. She's about a head taller than me, but she's skinnier. Her school jumper is baggy and not tucked up at all, and you can tell that she's completely, totally flat. When I look down at my own chest, I'm not exactly thrilled with what I see. Or don't see. But at least there are two little bumps that show some promise for the future.

I wonder if the boys noticed that, even as I remind myself that the hot list is stupid and cruel.

'Hannah helped me, you know.' Alice is talking more quietly now, like she finally gets that I might not want everyone to hear us. 'So if you need help …'

Alice keeps talking, but I drift off, thinking about the list again. Hannah didn't even make the list. There are forty-four girls in our year, so four haven't made the list at all, including Hannah. She went to the same primary school as Alice and me. She's kind of fat, but it's not just fat under her school polo. It's as if she 'developed' too quickly, and she's trying to hide it. In primary school, 'developing' was embarrassing. Hannah was the first girl, by ages, to get her period. Everyone knew, because she would only go into the one toilet cubicle that had a sanitary dispenser thing.

I would have hated to get my period way before anyone else, but it's really stressing me out that I still haven't got it now. I'm thirteen and four months, and … nothing's happening.

I sneak a sideways glance at Alice as she chats away. I wonder if she has hers yet.

Olympia skids across the floor between me and Alice. Her hand is on her locker door, but her eyes dart up the hallway to where Edi is.

'Hi, Hazel,' she says, ignoring Alice.

She grabs her maths book and slams the locker door as though she's in a hurry. But we've got plenty of time to get to maths.

'I'm walking with Edi,' she calls over her shoulder as she dashes ahead. 'You and Alice can talk maths together.'

I smile. On the outside. But inside it feels like a little stab. Olympia is part of my group, but she says stuff like this to me all the time. Cutting stuff. She must've heard Alice going on about homework. I would've liked to walk with her and Edi – they're in my group, after all.

That's the thing with Olympia. I'm not even sure if she was trying to be mean or if it just came out that way. Sometimes she's really nice to me. One thing I *am* sure about is that Olympia takes every opportunity to get Edi to herself. But I guess Jess and I are a bit like that too.

Edi is number one on the hot list, and she's number one in our group, too. That's just how it is.

'You go ahead if you like, Hazel,' Alice says.

For a second, I think about leaving Alice behind and

catching up to Edi and Olympia. But I can't. It would look too try-hard, for one. And secondly, it would be mean to Alice.

Even from the back, you can see why Edi is number one on the list. I would have put her there as well. Her mum is Indian, and Edi has long dark hair that she straightens even though she doesn't really need to. It really gleams, and her eyes do too. Even the braces on her teeth look good, like a little bit of extra jewellery you can't get told off for wearing. Plus, she's incredibly cool. I was with Edi when we saw the hot list for the first time. She rolled those eyes like it was no big deal. That's how cool she is.

Alice and I are just about to walk up the portable stairs when Nicholas Bradbury flies down them. I think he's definitely going to knock us over, but he just manages to stop in time.

'Morning, Hazel! Morning, Alice!' he says, his whole face screwing up with his grin.

'Morning, Nick,' we say together.

I don't know how he does it, maybe it's his Down syndrome, but Nick stretches his grin even wider and launches into the song we've been learning for music performance. He sings loud and strong and over-the-top, using his fist as a microphone like he's on stage.

His free arm waves about so much that Alice and I have to lean back.

'I'm going to do that homework tonight,' I whisper to Alice as Nick sings. 'If I get stuck, I'll message you, yeah?'

There's a smile between us that makes me glad I've said it. It's a *how weird is life? Can you believe how much has changed?* exchange, and Nick has caused it somehow.

I can tell Alice loves Nick as much as I do. I think it's the fact that he doesn't worry about all the stuff everyone else worries about. He's just really *honest,* I guess.

Alice gives me a little nod as the three of us break into the chorus, Nick's voice ringing out over the top of ours. Laughing, Alice and I head up the stairs, waving goodbye to Nick, who sees some other students and backtracks.

In D12, Edi, Jess and Olympia are sitting at a hexagonal table at the back of the room. They are leaning towards each other, plotting something. When she sees me, Jess jumps up and almost runs over.

,

'Saved you a seat, Haze,' she says breathlessly, threading her arm through mine.

'Cool,' I reply, though Jess saving me a seat is nothing out of the ordinary. What is strange, though, is her expression. She looks pleased with herself when she smiles. Something's behind the smile. I know there's news. It's almost bursting out of her.

I feel Alice peel off me. I can see her scanning her options before she takes a seat next to Erin and Briana at the front. It's not like anything gets said, like there are any spoken rules about who sits where, but I know if Alice sat at our table, the others would think it was wrong.

Alice hasn't got how to fold her jumper up the right way, and she doesn't know not to act too keen about homework, but she's got this right.

'Oh my god,' Jess says, as she practically pushes me into my seat. She leans forward. Edi and Olympia do the same, so I copy.

'All right,' Edi says, 'whatever you've got happening tonight, cancel it. Caravan meeting, five o'clock.'

Olympia nods as she sits back in her chair. 'Yeah, I'm

skipping basketball. This is more important.'

'Why? What's up?' I ask.

I love our caravan meetings, but they're normally on Friday so we can go through everything that's happened during the week. Something extra important is obviously going on for a Tuesday meeting, and it seems that I'm the only one who doesn't know what it is.

Mr Cartwright walks in.

'I'll tell you tonight,' Jess whispers, as Nick closes the door behind Mr Cartwright like he's royalty.

Mr C is pretty strict. You're not allowed to talk to each other during class unless it's about work, but Jess squeezes in a few more words before he begins the lesson.

'Do I look any different?' she asks, posing for me by flicking her ponytail and jutting out a shoulder.

I don't quite know what to say. Jess doesn't look any different to me, but that's obviously not what she wants to hear. I do a quick scan, checking her hair, face, clothes. Nup, no signs of difference.

Luckily it's too risky to reply anyway. Mr C can really crack it and I hate being told off.

Suddenly I get it. It's like a weight that lands in my chest and sinks down into my tummy.

I'm pretty sure I know what the meeting's going to be about.

GIRL _{OF THE} WORLD

I Heart you

Archie De Souza

• CHRISSIE PERRY •

COMING SOON!

Edi's got great friends and good grades, but that's not enough to satisfy her parents. Her whole family are doctors and lawyers, and she's expected to follow in their footsteps. No pressure! Worst of all, her mum and dad barely pay attention to her – except to tell her to study harder. If only they knew her favourite subject is her crush, Archie de Souza.

When Edi and Archie hook up, Edi can hardly believe her luck. Soccer-mad Archie is gorgeous and funny, and his loving family welcome her with open arms. Finally, she feels like she's surrounded by people who love her just the way she is. But is Archie more interested in sport than he is in Edi?

GIRL vs the WORLD

Girls, Guys and Choc-Cherry Pies

MEREDITH BADGER

Athletics star Leni is totally confused. She's trained with her friend Adam for ages, so why has he started acting really strangely around her? And since when is her bestie, Anya, so interested in boys that she's organised a kissing competition? Worse still, Anya's forcing Leni to take part. There's no-one Leni's even remotely into – and besides, she'd rather hang out with Jo, the new girl at school.

Jo's cool and fun and really seems to understand Leni. But as their friendship grows, Leni starts wondering if they might be more than friends. Maybe there is someone she'd like to kiss after all ...

Thalia Kalkipsakis grew up on a farm on the outskirts of Melbourne. After a stint as a dancer, she worked as an editor, but her biggest passion has always been writing. She is the author of numerous short stories, non-fiction titles and novels, including the YA novel *Silhouette* and the *Lifespan of Starlight* YA trilogy, as well as many books within the best-selling *Go Girl* series.